There Go I

BILL VANPATTEN

Publisher's Note: These stories are works of fiction. The names, characters, situations, places, and other elements of each story are creations of the author's imagination or are used fictitiously. Any resemblance to actual persons, alive or dead, events, or locales is unintended and coincidental.

Copyright © 2022 by Input and More, LLC,
and Bill VanPatten

All rights reserved. Published in the United States by Input and More, LLC, Chowchilla, CA. Any reproduction and/or distribution of this work without permission of the publisher is subject to the copyright laws of the United States.

Cover and interior design by KUHN Design Group.

ISBN 979-8-3543-8616-1

Printed in the United States through
Amazon Kindle Direct Publishing.

ALSO BY BILL VANPATTEN

Sometimes You Just Know

A Little Rain

Looks Are Deceiving
(A Will Christian Mystery)

Seidon's Tale

Dust Storm:
Stories from Lubbock

The Whisper of Clouds:
Stories from the Windy City

Ángel (in Spanish)

Elena (in Spanish)

Daniel (in Spanish)

Cuentos cortos (in Spanish)

PRAISE FOR BILL VANPATTEN'S WORK

FOR *LOOKS ARE DECEIVING*

"A top-notch, deliciously readable mystery…"
—*The Prairies Book Review*

"A cozy mystery/thriller with an unlikely and admirable hero, and a meaningful message…Loved it!"
—*Reedsy Discovery*

"A highly readable whodunnit that's well grounded in social issues."
—*Kirkus Reviews*

"A well-executed mystery with an engaging main character. There are enough twists and turns to keep the reader guessing who the killer is. The subject of racism is impactful and stays with you long after you've finished the book."
—*Writer's Digest 2021 e-Book Competition*

"VanPatten delivers a compelling and simply unexpected story that reveals how psychopathic minds work. Fans of mystery crime novels will definitely love it."
—*Readers' Favorite (Five Stars)*

"…by grounding a fictional work in reality, author VanPatten lends serious weight and stakes to his novel, transforming a simple mystery into a work of important cultural commentary, which is a rare feat in the genre."
—*Self-Publishing Review (Four Stars)*

"VanPatten keeps the cat-and-mouse murder mystery plot in constant motion in Looks Are Deceiving, gradually accelerating the pace as it moves closer to amateur investigator Will Christian solving the crimes."
—*IndieReader (4.8 Stars)*

"…this is a terrific roller-coaster ride that readers will find immersive."
—*BlueInk Review*

FOR *SEIDON'S TALE*

"Following the lead of authors like Madeline Miller and Rick Riordan, who pen modern mythology-based fiction so well, Seidon's Tale depicts Poseidon as a complex but kindhearted god who loves his brothers and sisters almost to a fault."

—Kops-Fetherling Silver Phoenix Award, 2019

"The pacing is fantastic and the narrative flows effortlessly. Lovers of Greek mythology will love these never-before-explored sides of the gods and their very human emotions."

—27th Annual Writer's Digest Self-published Book Awards

"The author flawlessly weaves fantasy and realism in a way that recalls Neil Gaiman's American Gods, breathing life into ancient mythology and bringing significance to Jake's empty modern existence…The fast-paced action throughout the book leads to a meaningful and satisfying ending for the characters and readers alike."

—The US Review of Books

FOR *A LITTLE RAIN*

"…a textbook slow-burn storyline…"

—Readers' Favorite (5 stars)

"An emotional, reflective, and engrossing novel. A Little Rain is a melancholy exploration of the unfortunate effects of discrimination and denial, for a story loaded with import and meaning that is conveyed with sensitivity, without being overly blunt or sentimental. All told, this is a stellar family drama with a compelling mix of contemporary issues, powerfully emotive writing, and twist-driven mystery."

—Self-Publishing Review (5 stars)

"A psychological thriller…VanPatten's A Little Rain delves deep into what makes its characters tick."

—The Indie Reader (5 stars)

To Mark Spencer

Table of Contents

· · ·

There Go I	13
Leaving	21
At the Bar	27
Malcontent	41
Loss	51
The Night Before	61
Buzz	71
Dark	83
Dawn	95
Noche Buena	103
Home	111
Beneath	121
Elena	133

"People aren't either wicked or noble. They're like chef's salads, with good things and bad things chopped and mixed together in a vinaigrette of confusion and conflict."

LEMONY SNICKET, *The Grim Grotto*

"Life is what happens to us while we are making other plans."

ALLEN SAUNDERS

"That, my dear, is what makes a character interesting, their secrets."

KATE MORTON, *The Forgotten Garden*

There Go I

She wore bitterness like it had been carved into her face by a mad sculptor. Each wrinkle, each line in her advanced crow's feet, each gin blossom bore witness to a heart that long ago must have stopped feeling anything other than resentment. Her peppered hair was untamable in its greasy need to flop back and forth with each lumbering step. An oversized T-shirt blared "Chukchansi Casino." Faded blue jeans hugged her double-wide hips. I imagined her as a homeless person—straddling the gap somewhere between menopause and old-age dementia—pushing a shopping cart along the street, yelling at passersby, and flipping the bird to anyone who honked at her to get out of the way. But here, inside the Save Mart, in the produce section, she was just a local shopper scowling at oranges and apples.

I'd heard rumors. In our gated community there was an abundance of storytellers. Danny, for example, was all of twenty-one years old and had grown up in the neighborhood. Wheelchair-bound since the age of thirteen, he'd lived his life through everyone else's business, making it his mission to know all the news, all the dirt. I guess when your world is reduced in scope and accessibility, your desire for gossip becomes insatiable.

"She's cray cray," he once told me. "Her ex-husband told the judge, 'Give her everything—the house, the car—I don't care. Just get the bitch out of my life.'"

Danny's eyes lit up as he recounted this tidbit, wanting to pull me into his eddied existence of others' lives. Being in my mid-forties, I knew enough to understand Danny's motivation. He was attracted to older men, but like so many in the town of Mañana, he confined his desires to occasional faceless postings on Grindr, a confession he made to me one day in whispered tones.

"I just wanted you to know we have something in common," he'd said, eyes twinkling.

As he spoke of the woman and her divorce, I knew that in his mind, dishing on others would make us friends, cause me to like him. I did, but at best as a teacher might like a slower student in class—that kind of friendliness that fuses fondness with pity.

"And guess what," he added. "The ex-husband died a year later. She remarried and got divorced again after just five years. I hear he's on his deathbed, too."

I nodded as he chatted, wondering how much was true. But the head security guard confirmed this woman was beyond just a screw loose, that maybe the hinges were about to give way.

"Neighbors called us out a number of times," he said, his six-foot, uniformed bulk lending authority to his voice. "Once she wielded a baseball bat and wouldn't let her husband into the house. Then there was the time she tried to run over the bastard in the driveway." He spat onto the lawn next to the guard shack. "Yeah, she's got more issues than *People* magazine."

* * *

I stood in front of the array of avocados, squeezing several in the pretense of selecting one. She moved over to the mushrooms and began inspecting them, picking each one up, turning it over and sniffing. I pictured her behind the wheel of her big-ass Buick, throwing it into gear and aiming for her husband—like a deranged Kathy Bates character. Had she headed straight for him, foot slammed on the accelerator, wanting to ram his gut? Or had she aimed for the knees with the intent to cripple him for life?

I glanced down at the avocados and considered their thick, parchmented skins, their soft flesh underneath that could ravish your tongue like a buttery lover, and their impenetrable pits the size of a small, unbeating heart. Inside this woman—with her baseball bat, with her husband-gunning car—was there something soft and buttery? Or was she just a tough, crinkled exterior wrapped around a stone-like pit? I looked up at her. *What brought her to this point?* I asked myself.

Such questions always got me to thinking. We are, after all, a sum of our life's experiences. When I was ten, I had already figured out that boys were more appealing to me than girls. My uncle must have sensed this, perhaps from watching the way I walked, the way I talked, the way I played. He slipped into my room one night as he babysat me and my sister, softly perching himself on the side of the bed. He stroked my head and asked why I spent so much time alone.

"I dunno," I whispered.

It was dark and although my parents weren't home, something told me I should speak in hushed tones. Moonlight filtered through the window, its pale bluish-white glow illuminating his hand as it moved from my head to my cheek, his knuckles barely brushing against me as he let his hand drift toward my chest.

"I think I know why," he said, hints of Old Spice and beer coming off of him.

His hand slid underneath the bed linens to rest on my belly. Slowly, his fingers probed for the elastic top of my pajama bottoms. I think I let out a slight moan because he leaned forward and put his lips to my ear.

"You know you're my favorite nephew," he cooed. "I would never hurt you."

* * *

The woman put the bag of selected mushrooms into her cart and headed for the deli section. I watched as several people passed by and nodded politely, none of them stopping to chat. She pushed on without acknowledging them. Her uneven gait caused me to glance down. Her feet were clad in scuffed white Nikes, the heels worn on the sides, her ankles thick like baby sequoias growing up into a pale denim shroud. Why did she have a slight limp? Was it from a row with her ex-husband? Or was it the scar of a long-ago injury, a constant reminder of some childhood trauma, like a bike accident or maybe something worse?

She stopped by the open case that held imported cheeses. She didn't strike me as a brie kind of person or even a gouda lover—her looks and demeanor suggested Velveeta was more to her taste or, at best, American sliced singles. She picked up a wrapped hunk of Swiss, maybe a Jarlsberg, examined the label, and then tossed it back among its kin. Something about that gesture—perhaps the cavalier loft she gave the cheese before it landed with a thump back in the display case—made me wonder if she had children and if she'd been a good mother, once had kindness in her eyes, or whether her kids grew up like unwanted items at the deli, tossed aside as powerless witnesses to the battles between their warring parents. Had CFS ever visited? Had neighbors ever checked in on the children? How had they grown up and what were their lives like now?

* * *

By the time I was thirteen, my uncle had begun to pass me around to his friends. I was popular because I was small, tallness not being a gene that had made its way to my parents' families—and those towering men liked to call me "son" and "boy" as they performed the three f's they relished with salivating eyes: fondling, fingering, and fucking. It never hurt. My uncle had trained me, I knew how to relax, and in that lonely space we nostalgically refer to as childhood, I liked the attention.

When I turned fifteen, my uncle found someone new, a younger cousin of mine. He was eleven, and I became the cast-off cheese, tossed back into the pile in the deli case. My uncle and I fought, and when I threatened to expose him, he slapped and punched me.

"Ungrateful!" I remember how he hissed when he spoke.

That night, I loaded his Tecate up with Seconal I'd gotten on the street, and he collapsed trying to fuck my little cousin.

The details of the aftermath of my uncle's sudden death aren't important. I'm here, my cousin's fine, and no one is the wiser. What is important is that we all have something we carry around, demons we exorcise on a daily basis. For some of us, what's inside gets turned into useful energy, creativity even. Van Gogh became a painter. Oprah became a celebrity icon. I became a writer. For others, what lurks inside festers, morphing into an emotional syphilis that blocks choices and stifles any chance at normalcy. Who knows why some of us go one way and others go another?

There Go I

* * *

I followed the woman as she made her way down the meat aisle. Again, she picked up a package, examined it and frowned, then tossed it back. She pushed on, the wheels of her shopping cart now squeaking, announcing her approach. I watched as the gaze of a five-year-old boy followed her turn into the bread aisle, knowing that he had not yet developed the adult restraint to keep from staring, his jaw slack as though he were taking in some manifestation of a monster he'd heard about from an older sibling.

This woman was not one of the lucky ones. I knew that whatever had happened to her had taken root like bad ivy and choked out anything that could bloom hope, and as her cart squeaked its way past loaves and buns neatly lined up on shelves, a voice spoke to me and said, *Enough, stop looking, this is not you.* Yet, it could have been. How many gay teenage kids, victims of abuse, wind up on the streets? How many stumble down a path of dark alleys and married johns pulling up in their family cars, emptiness pushing those teens to open the passenger door and slide in? How many die alone on filthy mattresses with needle marks in their arms?

I thought of twenty-one-year-old Danny and what he would do if he knew anything about my childhood, about my uncle—how he might telegraph my story from his wheelchaired existence.

* * *

As I emptied the grocery bag, my husband came up and put his arms around my waist. He hugged me.

"How was the grocery store?"

"Fine. Uneventful, as usual. How do nachos with guacamole sound?"

"Mmm."

He kissed me on the ear and then said he was going back to his office to finish something. I pulled out the avocados from the bag and stared at their wrinkled skin, picturing the hard pits within.

Leaving

He adjusts the focus with the hint of a twist, squinting into the eyepiece.

"You're right," he says, "that's Jupiter, not a star."

I want to say, "I told you so." Instead, I look at the stretched out inkiness above, perforated with the tiniest of diamonds, and I know that some are stars, some are planets, and some are galaxies. I could name many of them for him, but I don't. He would just think I was showing off. And I probably would be.

I zip up my hoodie, glad I layered before we left the house. I don't know if there is a real chill in the air or if it's just the slackening of my blood flow. Last night I read on a message board that terminally ill people often feel cold. Day by day, hour by hour, minute by minute, our bodies silently slip toward the final shut down.

I haven't told him I'm sick. He's my husband, and most would say he has a right to know. But he doesn't. He'll find out when he needs to find out. I suck in some of the mountain air, letting the scent of pine tickle my nostrils and enter my lungs. I want my ashes scattered up here. The sky is so clear at night. I could look up at the stars for all eternity. Well, not for all eternity. Even the universe will die someday. But not anytime soon.

He swivels the telescope to aim it in another direction.

"It's all so vast," he says as he bends over once more to peer through the lens. "It's humbling."

Yes, I think, the universe is vast, and it is humbling. If he only knew that I am going to leave this place by the age of forty-one, that a four-decade life is nothing compared to a 13-billion-year-old universe, and that on this tiny planet in a spiraling arm of the Milky Way, we are invisible.

And yet, we are here.

My husband and I have been together for ten years. I think the last two have been out of habit. I knew by the sixth year we would never celebrate a silver anniversary. His last affair was the one I couldn't forgive, the one that smashed into me like an asteroid striking the Earth. I had no fight left in me, couldn't do the work of saving our relationship anymore. That was six months ago. I was going to leave him, but my test results offered me a different kind of exit.

I study him as he once again maneuvers the telescope to a different spot in the sky. He is movie-star handsome-a Matt Bomer look-alike with dark hair and blue eyes, toned, hand-made by God for Armani. He is an architect and, by all accounts, a catch. My friends all told me so at the beginning. I'd had boyfriends before, but he was the one I fell in love with, the one who exalted me, made me feel as attractive as he was. I ate it all up, gobbled every "I love you" because I was hungry for words that would break the shackles of insecurity forged from a broken childhood.

"I see something that looks like a galaxy," he says. "Come here and tell me if I'm right."

I step toward him and close one eye while I press the other against the rubber cup of the eyepiece. I tell him yes, he's right, it's Andromeda—named after the maiden chained to the rock to be ravaged by the sea monster Cetus. She was saved by Perseus, who descended from the sky on the back of Pegasus, ready with sword and Medusa's head. The irony doesn't escape me that I'm chained to this rock hurtling through space. But I will die on this rock. I will not be rescued.

I've already lost ten pounds, but he hasn't noticed. My doctor says that I will lose more. The cancer that worms its way around my organs will continue to suppress my appetite. I will begin to look sallow, and my skin will sag. I've declined all treatments. Why prolong the inevitable to gain a few months? What I'd like is another forty years-another four decades so that I can leave my Matt Bomer husband, take everything that's mine and start over, have a happy ending, find a Perseus.

Living well is often the best revenge.

But I don't have the time or luxury to live well. My revenge is to draw up a will in which everything that is mine is left to a foundation, to dictate the terms of my body's disposal, to leave all of this in the hands of my cousin, to take all the power over my death away from him. I want to die in front of him, take one last look into his eyes and then whisper into his ear, "It's over. I'm leaving you."

Sometimes, dying well is the best revenge.

I took up astronomy when I was ten. I was an only child in a failed marriage, my father abandoned us to take up with a woman at work. They moved to Seattle, and I never saw him again. I became the son he never wanted, the boy he couldn't love. My mother turned to drinking, and by the time I was fourteen, I'd become an expert at putting her to bed, cleaning up the occasional vomit, and hiding our life from friends and neighbors. Alone in the dark, the nighttime sky called to me. With my mother passed out somewhere in the house, I'd slip outside and lie on the grass, looking up at the heavens. I used books from the library to learn which stars were which, and what planets I could see with the naked eye. I got my first telescope when I turned sixteen, my PhD in astrophysics by the time I was twenty-six.

And now, four months past my fortieth birthday, I find myself at six-thousand feet above sea level at the edge of the Sierras. I watch my husband as he pretends to take interest in something I love. I think about what will happen to me, how the stars are the source of all life, and how I will give mine back to them. My molecules will rise into the air, be carried off to other parts of California, maybe beyond, and become part of this planet. Someday, the sun-our very own star-will expand and swallow the Earth, and I will have fulfilled the destiny of every living and non-living thing: to give back to the stars, give back to the universe.

"You look cold," he says.

I nod and he says it's time to pack it up and head home. I let him disassemble the telescope and place it in the back of our BMW. I lift my head, take in more of the pine scent, and let my gaze sweep across the expanse of night. It still beckons me, telling me it's waiting for me.

I will be part of a star. Someday.

At the Bar

She sat at the short end of the L-shaped bar, gazing at her drink. She appeared to be alone. I couldn't help staring at her. Not because she was a beauty, although she wasn't unattractive. Her wavy brown hair and blue eyes were the kind that would always get my attention. A number of my past girlfriends had dark hair and blue eyes. Even my soon-to-be ex-wife. But this woman at the bar—there was something about her, something different. I was intrigued, but still not ready to make a first move.

She looked up at me and I quickly cast my gaze down. Seconds ticked off and I forced myself to keep my eyes locked on the scotch in front of me. I swirled the ice cubes around and watched them chase each other in a teasing circle. After some time, I raised my head and brought the glass to my lips so that I could steal another furtive glance at her. She combed through her purse, finally pulling out an iPhone. She looked at the screen and smiled. Maybe she wasn't so alone after all. Maybe she was waiting for someone who was late.

Her thumbs flew across the screen. That's when I focused on her hands. They almost seemed too big for her. They were far from delicate—and certainly not small like my ex's hands. When I knew I was going to propose, I snuck one of her rings out of her bedroom and took it to a jeweler. He remarked that my girlfriend's hands must've been on the smaller side, and I shrugged, saying I guessed so. When he double-checked the size, he said yep, a size five like he'd thought. Turns out the average for women is size seven.

The woman at the bar was no size-seven ring. I scanned the hands of the few ladies who flanked me, and all were smaller than hers. I looked in her direction. She was still texting, her face down. I didn't want her to catch me, so I pretended to study the room, taking in my dimly lit surroundings. I was in a restaurant bar: dark wood, long granite counter, nicer than a dive but not quite on par with a bar in the Four Seasons or The Peninsula. Soft music floated among the din of voices that surrounded me.

As usual, I was by myself. I hadn't dated much since my split. I had slid into a late-thirties slump with forty just months away—wisps of gray creeping at my temples, silently signaling what my dad had called the Slow Decline. But what had really set me down the path of drinks-alone-at-the-bar in the middle of the week was the divorce. My ex had left me for a guy I'd worked with. They'd been having an affair for almost a year. One day she came home and told me it was adios, muchacho. Well, she didn't say it like that.

"Adam, I'm not gonna beat around the bush," she'd said as she slung her gym bag onto a stool at the kitchen counter.

I'd been making dinner. Pasta with marinara sauce and Portobello mushrooms. One of her favorite dishes. I looked at her, trying to read her face, but nothing in her expression offered me a clue. And before I could ask what was up, she said, "I'm leaving. I'm in love with someone else." Just like that. *I'm in love with someone else.* She might as well have said we were low on milk or that she had a doctor's appointment the next day.

It wasn't until later that it hit me—like someone had pulled the plug in my bathtub of normalcy and my life glug-glug-glugged its way down a dark drain and off into the sewer of broken hearts. For several days, I was a zombie until I realized I needed to quit that job and find a new one. How could I stay when my wife's lover was a few steps down the hallway from me? I'm not prone to violence but I had visions of marching into his office, picking up his laptop, and slamming it into his head. Crack! Like a fucking watermelon with the juices oozing out. Yeah, so I had to leave. It wasn't too hard to find something new in software development. Within a week, I was out of there and headed for a new position a few miles away in Fresno.

So here I was on a Wednesday night six months later, propped on a stool in a bar with a scotch to keep me company. I hadn't fully developed the scars to cover my wounds, but I was making progress. Oh sure, I was drinking alone. But at least now I was curious about someone else, wasn't I?

I let my gaze crawl along the walnut paneling of the walls to the neatly lined-up bottles behind the bar, the low hum of conversations in the background reminding me there were other people there. I continued to peruse, first the handles on the beer pulls, then the trays of lime and lemons wedges snuggled next to the maraschino cherries. Finally, I focused on the woman once more. Shit. She was staring at me. I didn't know what to do, so I just smiled. She smiled in return. Just then Jake, the bartender, showed up. He gestured with his head toward my almost empty glass.

"Ready for another?"

"Sure," I said. "It's only my first."

He looked at me oddly, then turned to look at the woman

down the bar, then back at me. He said nothing and went about pouring a fresh drink for me. Clearly, he'd seen us both make eye contact. I debated asking him whether she was a regular and if he knew her, but a patron signaled him for another round, and he was off.

I pretended to look around for someone and saw the woman once again looking intently at her phone screen. I watched those thumbs move at a fairly quick speed. While her head was down, I took the time to take more of her in. Although she was seated, she seemed on the tall side—at least if you compared her to the people around her. I imagined her a volleyball player in college—great at the net, and with those hands, a powerhouse server. I remembered a girl at the university who was on the team. They could have been sisters. And then I noticed her breasts tucked away inside a light blue satin blouse. They seemed small, I mean, for her height anyway. I've never been a big-boobs guy. I'm not one of those men whose eyes go straight for the cleavage when meeting a woman, and I don't care what cup size a woman is. Oh, I'll watch Pamela Anderson run on the beach in Baywatch. Who wouldn't? But someone like Dolly Parton just isn't natural. So, boobs aren't the first thing I go for. I don't think there is a first thing I go for. Well, maybe dark hair and blue eyes. Like my ex. My thoughts were interrupted when the woman stopped texting, picked up her drink, and looked over at me.

Damn it!

She smiled and this time she winked. Not a flirtatious wink but an I-caught-you-looking wink. I was thankful for the quasi-dim lighting because I'm sure I'd turned red. I half-smiled, winked back, and then took a sip of my drink so that I could divert my gaze. Out of the corner of my eye, I saw her get up and I thought she was going to come over to my side of the bar. I shifted in my seat. But instead of approaching, she headed for the restroom. I watched her saunter away, taking in her clipped gait and the slim hips and small but rounded butt covered in Levi denim as it disappeared into the far side of the restaurant. Jake came into my view.

"I saw you checking Jessie out," he said.

"I wasn't checking anyone out." I let my vision focus on my drink.

"Sure," he said with a tone dripping with disbelief.

I looked up. "But now that you're here, I'm curious. Is she a regular?"

"Yep. Been coming in since before I started working here."

"Is she always alone?"

"Nope. Sometimes with a girlfriend. Never with a guy."

I pondered this. "Well, that's interesting."

"Probably a reason for that," Jake added.

"What would that be?"

He folded his arms onto the bar and leaned in close. He lowered his voice. "Not many guys like to be with a woman who used to be a man."

"What?"

Jake smiled. "Come on! You can tell. Jessie used to be a guy. Hell, maybe she still is. You know. Hasn't had the snip yet."

Another patron called out to Jake and I was left there, mouth open. A guy? This woman used to be a guy? I took a big gulp of scotch. Did that explain the large hands? The smallish boobs? Images eddied in my head. Dark hair. Blue eyes. Smiles. I was attracted to her. I'd winked at her.

Shit.

I took another gulp of scotch. I focused on her empty spot and jumped when I felt a hand on my shoulder.

"Hey, dude, why so edgy?" It was Bryan, a coworker. A big smile stretched across his face.

"God, Bro. You scared the shit out of me. What're you doing here?"

"Hump day," he said and signaled to Jake.

"You come here a lot?" I asked.

"On occasion."

Jake showed up with a vodka martini. Bryan took a sip and sighed. "Ah, I love a good drink at the end of the day."

"So, where's David?"

David was Bryan's fiancé. Bryan had proposed to him in an elaborate flash-mob scene at Oracle Park during a home game. They were big-time Giants fans and known to host great baseball-watching parties. How the hell Bryan had pulled off that proposal on the Giants' field I'd never know. When I proposed to my ex, we were at a sunset barbecue, and I got down on my knee- old school and very simple. Bryan knew how to do things big.

"He had to go to Seattle for business. He'll be back on Friday." Bryan looked at me over the rim of his glass, giving me the once over. "So, what's up with you?"

"What'd'ya mean?"

He put his glass down. "Adam, you jumped when I touched you. You've been looking around since I got here. Off and on you look down at your drink. I mean really. I don't need to be Hercule Poirot to notice something's got you preoccupied."

Before I could answer, Jessie returned. She took her seat, and when she looked up at us, her face beamed.

"Oh!" Bryan said. "I have to go say 'hi' to someone. Back in a minute." With martini in hand, he made his way toward her. *Oh fuck. Does he know her?* When he reached Jessie, he leaned in and gave her a light kiss on the cheek. They hoisted glasses and clinked. As they talked, I wished I could overhear their conversation. There were a few laughs and Jessie tossed her hair back as she looked over at me again.

I looked away so fast that I got those little zig-zag lines that appear when we change our focus too quickly. I blinked and shook my head. When I got the nerve to sneak a peek in their direction, they were engaged in a serious discussion. I wondered if it was about me. They didn't glance over at me while talking, but then maybe one told the other not to look. I could only imagine her asking Bryan who I was, how he knew me, if I was single. Surely, he would tell her I was finalizing a divorce. Did I want her to know anything about me after what Jake had said? Bryan leaned in for one more kiss on the cheek and then I watched him leave her to make his way back to me. Again, I focused on my drink, not wanting Bryan to catch me looking. I studied the ice cubes as they lay there in my glass, half-melted. Bryan appeared by my side and took an empty seat.

"So," he said, "what's up with you since I last saw you at the staff meeting this morning?" When I looked up, his hazel eyes bore into me.

"Not much." I sounded like some guy in a locker room, uncommitted to the substance of the conversation. "Megan sent me an email. The escrow went through on the condo sale, so I'll finally get my share of the money."

Bryan raised his glass. "Mazeltov."

I swished the scotch in my glass. "Uh, how well do you know Jessie?"

He arched an eyebrow. "You know her?"

I gestured at Jake the Bartender with a head movement.

"Oh," Bryan said, "the resident one-man gossip chain. What did he tell you?"

"Well…" I cleared my throat. "Jake seems to think…well, I dunno…he said…" I looked down at my ice cubes again. They were beginning to shrivel.

"Yeah?" Bryan nudged.

"Well, he thinks that Jessie used to be a man."

Bryan just nodded as though he were contemplating what I'd said. After a pause, "And what do you think?"

"What do you mean 'What do I think?'"

I must have said this rather loud. Several people turned to look at me. I caught a glimpse of Jessie. Her head was once again focused on her phone as she thumbed a text.

"Dude," Bryan said, "chill."

I didn't say anything as I turned to look at him. He tilted his head slightly as he studied me.

"Does it make a difference if she's transgender?" he asked.

"Make a difference how?"

"I dunno. You brought it up."

We both sat in silence for a moment. Then Bryan said, "You're attracted to her, aren't you?"

"Fuck you," I muttered, once again avoiding his gaze, and letting my own vision settle on the drink cradled in my hands.

"Me thinks the lady doth protest too much," Bryan said.

There was another pause. When I finally looked up at him, he was staring at me. He arched an eyebrow again, and then he smiled. He took a sip of his martini without saying anything, all the time his gaze was locked on mine. The skewered olives in his glass moved from one side to the next, like they were waving to me, maybe taunting me.

"Look," I finally said. "You know me. We've been friends for a while. I'm not homophobic…"

He pounced on the suspension in my voice. "But?" Another sip of his martini.

I felt sweat in my armpits. Was I really having this conversation? My focus went back to the now puny ice cubes in my drink. Bryan must've noticed my discomfort.

"You ready for another?" he asked.

"I guess."

He signaled to Jake, and within seconds, another scotch and another martini appeared before us, almost as if Jake knew about our conversation and had the drinks ready.

"Adam," Bryan said, his voice soft, but with a slight edge. "There is a homophobia here. Deep down, something bugs you that you might be attracted to a woman who used to be a man. Even though she's a woman now. Something inside makes you question your sexuality."

That last comment stung. It was true that since my ex-wife had left, my confidence had wobbled and, yes, I had asked myself off and on what kind of man I was that my wife was no longer interested in me—why she preferred that dipshit I worked with. Was he a better lover? Had a bigger dick? Or had she simply grown tired of me and needed something new? Whatever the reason, my sense of masculinity had shrunk in half within a month of our separation. I was nothing, a throw away, unsatisfying to her. I shrugged off the thoughts, not wanting Bryan to see I had momentarily slipped into a mental minefield.

"If Jake hadn't said anything," he said, "what would you have done? No! Wait! If Jessie had come over here to talk to you, what would you have done?"

I cast my sight down one more time to hide in my drink, but the fresh ice cubes didn't help. Floating like little four-sided mirrors I could almost see myself in them, see the hesitation in my eyes, see the confusion.

"Adam, looking down at your drink tells me everything."

I sighed. "Look, Bryan. You know me. It's just…well…I've just never confronted this before."

I took a quick glimpse out of the corner of my eye. Jessie was still texting. At least she wasn't watching this conversation. Why did I care if she had been a man?

"Let me ask you this." I turned the tables on Bryan. "Would you be with Daniel if he'd been a woman before being Daniel?"

"Good question. But I'm not the one in your situation."

I looked him square in the eye. "Would you?"

He stirred the olives in the glass with an almost delicate, sensual motion and then brought them to his mouth. "Of course I would. I fell in love with him as a man."

The olives slipped behind his teeth. Two little orbs plucked away from their perch. Snip.

Just then, Jake walked by and gave me a wink. What the hell was that for? All of a sudden, I felt like all of the eyes in the bar were on me.

"I get it," Bryan said. "This whole transgender thing makes everyone question everything about sexuality, identity, attraction, politics, athletics…shit, even what bathroom to use. But the bottom line is this: you're attracted to Jessie because she's a woman. She's not a man."

He arched his eyebrows, inviting a response. I remained silent. He shrugged, then set his empty glass on the bar and signaled Jake for the check.

"These are on me," he said.

"No, you can't…"

"But I can, and I am," he said. "Listen. I'm gonna meet a friend for dinner. You wanna join?"

Part of me wanted to. Another part wanted to stay so that I could…could what? Catch glimpses of Jessie while she wasn't looking? Study her? Wonder about her? Bryan picked up on my hesitation.

"Okay," he said. "Stay here. If later you want to come to the dining area, just look for me. Talk to you later, Bro." He squeezed my shoulder, then left. I sat there for a while. A low buzz caught my attention. I looked down at my phone. My ex had just texted.

> Got one final doc. Can you sign by
> the end of the week?

It was perfunctory, as usual. No "How you doin'?" or "Hey. I gotta ask you something." Instead, straight up front.

I'm in love with someone else.

One final document. From now on, my life with Megan would be told in the past tense—and someday it would be nothing but a collection of memories, neural photos stored somewhere in my mental album. Something like a sigh tried to form in me but nothing came out. I texted back.

> Sure. I can do it during
> lunch on Friday.

I hit send. I downed another mouthful of my scotch, the conversation with Bryan dogging my thoughts. How did I really feel about Jessie? Or was I avoiding what I felt about myself? The divorce weighed on me. My soon-to-be ex had tossed me aside for someone else and I'd had no clue. I'd plummeted but slowly climbed back. And now, the first inkling of any desire was for a trans-woman. I just couldn't wrap my head around it. Yet, another part me called myself an asshole, that Bryan was right, maybe some kind of homophobia lurked within. Yes, this was Fresno. Yes, this was a more conservative part of California. But it was also the 21st century. Hadn't we moved beyond the labels? Hadn't I moved beyond them? A voice whispered to me that I hadn't. Another voice whispered that I'd found Jessie attractive.

"Shit," I muttered.

I took another sip. I could make an effort, I thought. At least make a new friend. Prove that I could do that at least, regardless of what Jessie was or wasn't or what other people thought. Yeah. I could do that. I'd use Bryan as my excuse: "I noticed you're friends with someone I work with, so…"

But when I looked over in her direction, she was gone. Jake had already picked up her glass and was wiping down the bar where she'd been sitting. I looked around. Nothing. I called Jake over.

"Hey, does Jessie come in every Wednesday?"

"Pretty much," he said.

I thanked him and he returned to his task. I looked down at the ice cubes in my glass one last time. If they could have smiled at me, I think they would have.

Malcontent

"Have you ever been in love?"

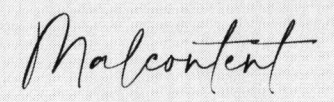

Shane eyed the interviewer, not having expected that question. They were there to talk about his writing, his latest collection of stories in particular. He'd recently been nominated for an important literary prize, and *Good Lines* magazine had sent a journalist out to interview him. Shane figured he was at least twice as old as the kid sitting across from him, maybe more. Jeremy Witherspoon—who had introduced himself with an added "no relation to the actress" line—couldn't have been out of college more than a couple of years. The kid didn't even have facial hair.

"How old are you?" Shane asked.

"Twenty-five. Why?"

Shane nodded, his lip curling up on one side, his mouth not sure whether it wanted to smile or smirk.

"Anyone your age would figure someone like me would have experienced lots of things in life. How the hell do you think I get my ideas?"

Jeremy cleared his throat.

"Mr. Matthews—"

"I already told you to call me Shane. Mr. Matthews was my father. And he's dead."

Jeremy twisted in his seat. "I was just following up on our conversation about your story 'Malcontent.' After all, it's a story about a broken man who isn't sure he's ever experienced love."

Shane looked around for the server. They were seated in Farnucci's—a pitiful excuse for a restaurant-bar in the town of Mañana. Built in the 1960s and never updated, it consisted of paneled walls, dingy linoleum, and red faux leather banquettes that had been worn thin from the thousands of overweight people squashing their fat asses into the booths. Greasy fried chicken and mac and cheese were the staples on the menu. He would have preferred The Fairway over by the golf course, but it was closed for renovations. A fly buzzed in front of him. He spotted the server and waved her over.

"I'd like another martini." He turned to Jeremy. "You want another wine?"

"I probably shouldn't."

"Come on. The round's on me."

Jeremy shrugged and said, "Okay." The server bustled off.

"To answer your question, yes, I've been in love. Do you want specifics? Want me to talk about sex? Whether I'm a top or a bottom or versatile? How much dick I've sucked?"

Jeremy squinted. "Are you playing with me?"

"This is your interview. I'm just going through the door that you opened."

There was a pause as the two men eyed each other. The server returned with their drinks.

"Would you gentlemen like anything else?"

Shane looked at Jeremy with his eyebrows raised. The young man shook his head.

"We're good, thanks," Shane said.

"Flag me down if you change your minds." The server hurried off into the kitchen.

Shane took a long sip of his martini. "A guy I dated introduced me to martinis. He was a gin drinker, probably an alcoholic, or at least a functional one. He'd sweat on the hot days and I could smell the gin coming out of his pores. I couldn't stand it. I prefer vodka. No odor there." He took another long sip.

"Was he your first love?"

Shane stared down at his drink, twirling the glass by the stem. He sighed. "No. No, he wasn't."

* * *

Randy was a boy in high school—a talented and musically gifted sixteen-year-old with dark hair and espresso-colored eyes, and a smile that could sell toothpaste. Shane had fallen hard and fast for him. They were junior-year lab partners in biology and by the end of the spring term, were best friends. Shane had kept his feelings to himself, mostly out of fear of rejection. The AIDs epidemic was front-page news, and the gay community was under siege by the self-proclaimed moralists with megaphones. Shane did not want to be labeled as a potential disease carrier.

But then one day over a Diet Pepsi at a local burger stand, Shane opened up.

"I have something to tell you," he said.

"What?"

Shane swallowed hard. "I wasn't sure if I should say anything. But I know now I have to."

Randy put his drink down. "What?" His tone had risen.

"I'm...I'm..." Shane drew in a deep breath. "I'm in love with you."

Randy's eye's widened, but Shane couldn't tell if it was from surprise or fear.

"I just had to tell you." Shane pleaded with his eyes.

"You're a fag?"

The question stung Shane into paralysis. Words formed in his head but never made it to his lips.

"So, you think I'm a fag, too?"

Shane's mouth finally moved. "Randy, that's not—"

The other boy shot up from his seat. "I'm not like that! Keep that shit away from me!" He hurried away, leaving Shane alone at the table.

For a week, Shane dragged himself to school, while his mother repeatedly asked him what was wrong and why he spent so much time in his room. He always replied, "Nothing." His stomach turned at the thought of telling her anything, Randy's use of the word "fag" echoing amid the chaotic images and feelings that plagued his thoughts. His dad approached him one night and sat on the edge of the bed.

"Son, your mom and I are worried."

"About what?"

His dad gazed at the floor before speaking.

"You don't seem yourself. You're…withdrawn."

"Dad, I'm fine. Really."

There was a pause before his dad looked at him squarely. "Is it drugs?"

"Oh, God. No!"

His dad nodded. "Is it a girl then? Something happen with a girl?"

Shane seized up inside but did his best not to show it.

"No. Honestly. There's nothing wrong."

His dad pursed his lips then patted him on the leg. "Well, if you ever want to talk, just let me know."

Even if he'd wanted to talk, Shane didn't. He kept his secret. For their entire senior year, he and Randy didn't speak. Day by day, he endured the mix of humiliation and loss, burying his feelings and waiting for the day high school would be behind him. June finally arrived and an incipient sense of relief bubbled within Shane. By the end of summer, as he prepared to leave for college, his life was back to normal. A decade later, he ran into Randy at a Barnes & Noble. Both were browsing the table marked 'Our Employee Picks.' When Shane looked across the array of books, his eyes widened in recognition. Randy smiled, came around to the other side, and hugged him.

"So, how's life?" Randy asked.

"Not bad," he responded. "I got a degree in English and creative writing, then my MFA."

"You're a writer?"

Shane nodded. "Fiction. I've published a few stories here and there. I'm working on a novel now. And teaching, of course."

Randy grinned. "Wow! I'm impressed."

Shane shrugged. "How about you?"

"Turned out I have an engineering streak in me. I work for a tech firm in San Jose." He paused. "I have something to tell you. I'm gay. I came out in college."

Shane's heart fluttered at the news. Internally, he stumbled over what to say. *Well, good for you,* came to mind, as did, *I guess I had you pegged back in high school.* He also considered *I still love you, you know.* Even, *And you're a shit for not looking me up in the meantime.* Nothing seemed appropriate, so he just smiled.

"I also have a boyfriend," Randy added. "We've been together for a year now."

Shane kept smiling to hide his disappointment. And then his mind went elsewhere, that he could bury his disappointment in a short story about lost love.

Timing sucked.

* * *

"Shane?"

Jeremy's voice yanked Shane from his reverie. He cleared his throat.

"Sorry. I was just thinking of a story I'm working on. Happens all the time."

Jeremy nodded. "Back to 'Malcontent.' I asked you about your own love because the protagonist doubts that love exists. The cliché is that we should write about what we know."

Shane stirred the toothpick with the skewered olives soaking in his now half-empty glass. From the kitchen, he heard voices—probably a pissed off cook and a co-working having words. The restaurant was still largely empty of customers. It was only three o'clock after all. He turned his gaze to Jeremy, looking directly into the young man's blue eyes.

"You're right that it's a cliché. Fiction is fiction for a reason."

"But you must draw on some kind of inspiration."

"Look, kid—"

"I'm not a kid." Jeremy's nostrils flared slightly. "I'd appreciate you not calling me that."

Shane held up his hands. "Sorry. Look, I've had relationships, and if you want to know the truth, none of them worked out."

Jeremy sipped on his wine and then leaned in. "I'm trying to prove myself at *Good Lines*. I want to get a good story from you, something that my boss will like. Otherwise, I'll wind up in the copyediting room the rest of my life."

Shane chuckled. "I figured as much, but I doubt you'll wind up in a backroom somewhere. You have a long life ahead of you and things can change before you know it."

He slugged down another mouthful of martini and stood.

"And besides, even though I think of you as a kid, you're not dumb. You'll have a successful career, I'm sure. Back in a second." He headed for the restroom.

He stood at the urinal, his mind a flood of thoughts and images…

* * *

Shane met Alan right after he'd turned thirty. He'd recently moved to Chicago for a job in creative writing at the University of Illinois, and the two men shared a table at a faculty orientation workshop on campus. At first, Shane wasn't sure if Alan was interested. Their initial meeting gave him no clues as to Alan's orientation. But they exchanged business cards to stay in touch. On a lark, he called Alan and invited him out for a drink. Shane had dated off and on over the years, but the most he'd lasted with any guy was six months. Something like hope floated within him when Alan accepted the invitation.

"I read your novel," Alan said as they sat at a local bar.

"Ha. You and twelve other people."

"You're a good writer."

Shane looked down at his drink.

"You are!" Alan said.

"Don't flatter me," Shane deadpanned. "It's the kind of talk that'll make me fall in love with you."

Alan was a good five inches taller than Shane and had dark hair and eyes that reminded him of Randy. After two dates, they wound up in bed, and nine months later, Alan moved in with Shane. Those early years were filled with passion. They were the fun times, the anticipated vacations, the days of sunshine and laughter. As time moved on, they settled into a routine, and after ten years, Shane realized the spark had gone out, even though he clung to the idea that romance was a real thing, not something made up by Hallmark and Nicholas Sparks. Then they hit the twelve-year mark, and Alan came home on a crisp early fall day and confessed he was seeing a twenty-year-old. Shane stared, slack jawed.

"What are you saying?" he finally said.

"It's over," was Alan's blunt reply.

Shane's pulse ticked up. "Just like that. It's over?"

Alan simply stared.

"How long has this been going on?"

"Six months."

Shane's face flushed. He stood. "What the fuck? You're old enough to be his dad!"

Alan didn't seem remorseful at all. He shrugged and said, "It's what I want."

Shane stormed out, went to a local bar, and downed a few drinks. An hour later, he returned to an empty home and found several suitcases missing and some of Alan's clothes no longer in the closet or drawers. He plopped onto the sofa and sobbed, his grief springing from the realization that love was an elusive thing, and that he was more afraid of being alone than of losing Alan. In his heart, he knew from the beginning that he'd conjured love in this relationship when it was nothing like what he'd felt for Randy years before.

Alan returned after several days to get the rest of his things, but Shane couldn't bear the thought of seeing him, so he spent the day with some friends at the Field Museum. As time progressed, he learned that Alan had been cheating on him almost since the beginning. The twenty-year-old wasn't the first.

So much for love.

Shane drifted from guy to guy over the next three years, most of them one-nighters. He stopped writing.

"I'm dried up," he told himself one day.

Needing a change, he took a job at Merced College and moved back to California when he turned forty-five. With a new environment and new students, came inspiration, and words flowed once again. On a whim, he decided to hunt Randy down after his first year back in the Golden State. He'd discovered in an online search that his high school crush had died of AIDs-related complications several years earlier. Shane spiraled into a mini depression. For a week, he couldn't write. He drank more than usual, and he cried himself to sleep every night.

Yeah, timing sucked.

After a few weeks passed, he got back to writing. He gave up looking for Mr. Right, if such a man even existed. The chances of getting into a relationship at his age were slim. His hair had already begun to gray at the temples and his waistline had grown several inches—the curse of sitting at computer so much during the day and drinking martinis every evening. The youth-obsessed gay subculture has passed him by, a train he'd gotten off, only to remain stranded in a station he didn't want to be at.

* * *

Shane flushed the urinal and watched as the water spilled down and curled around the drain, disappearing into the murky pipes below to mix with the piss and shit of countless strangers.

"Yeah. I've been in love," he muttered.

His thoughts turned to the young man who waited for him at the table. He'd been like him once. Eager. Ambitious. Even hopeful. And it occurred to him how his thoughts were cloaked in the past tense, like a finished story. Was it time to write something new?

He washed his hands and checked himself in the mirror. There were bags under his eyes and his crow's feet seemed to have gotten bigger over the last month. He hung his head and sighed. Then he straightened up and headed out, ready to give the interview the kid was hoping for.

Loss

Fog does not come on little cat feet. It snakes its way across the land, slithering down the San Joaquin Valley, a seductive killer cloaked in gray velvetiness prowling for victims. Silently it swallows everything in its path—a shopping center, a motel, a home. It creeps down highways and roads, obscuring the vision of lonely drivers, luring them deep into the mist. They know they should ease up and take their time. But many don't. They fall to the fatal charms of the fog and wind up a statistic, a news item at eleven o'clock, a fatality of a sexy predator. We bemoan tornadoes, hurricanes, and earthquakes—those devastating monsters that seize national attention as lead stories on tv and in print. But fog is silent and evades the headlines. Its stealth goes unheeded as local weather persons announce an advisory and then move on to the high and low temperatures for the day, the pollen count, and when the next rains will come.

    I stood at the kitchen window, the low hum of the refrigerator filling the space of my empty house. As I looked out, the fog formed a dense, vapored curtain obscuring the view of other homes. This mist would not burn off by noon. It would linger, cling to the ground with hungry intent. I sighed, turned, and headed toward my office. I'd already decided to work from home given the weather. I wasn't sure why I'd already dressed when I could have stayed in my sweats and a hoodie. We kept the house at seventy-two in the winter, my husband not abiding anything lower. And yet a chill settled on me. I reached up and rubbed my upper arms. Something pushed at my thoughts, a memory, but unlike the fog outside, it slipped away almost as soon as it had placed a toe on the threshold of my awareness. How odd. I shrugged it off and moved from the kitchen into the living room.

On my way, I stopped and looked at the array of photos on the sofa table. One of them was from my parents' wedding. I picked it up and studied their faces. They looked out with unsure expressions. Each offered a half-smile and eyes that should have sparkled with joy but didn't. And I wondered if, deep down, they knew on that day they'd end in divorce twenty-five years later. Some marriages are doomed from the outset, time chipping away at a shaky foundation built on impulse. They'd met at a Sonic drive-in. My dad was on leave from the military and my mother was a car hop in skimpy shorts and roller skates. Maybe she fell for the uniform and he for her legs. They were married six months later. I'm not sure how many times they tried to hurt or kill each other. I buried most of those memories. But like all buried memories, occasionally they rise to haunt you.

I set the photo down and picked up one of my brother Bobby. It was his high school graduation picture—his broad smile radiating the mix of pride and happiness at achieving one of life's earliest goals. In the photo, I saw myself. We were twins, born five minutes apart on a foggy December morning in Merced. No one could tell us apart except for our parents, and on occasion we'd fooled them too. Like many twins, we were close and shared our lives in ways that other siblings didn't. We both came out to each other at the same time, when we were sixteen. It turned out we had a crush on the same boy. You'd think we would've fought over him. But our bond was too thick, too hard for a boy to break. In the end, he was straight and married his high school sweetheart. Bobby and I laughed it off.

He met someone in college, at UC Davis. I'd gone to UC Santa Barbara. We'd decided to divide and conquer, not to fight after the same men on the same campus. One night he and his boyfriend were headed back to Davis from a party in Sacramento. A heavy fog had settled in, and his boyfriend slammed into the back of another car on I-80. Bobby died later in the hospital from head trauma. For some reason, he wasn't wearing his seat belt. I had a good hunch why. In spite of the weather, maybe because of the added danger, he was probably doing something naughty to his boyfriend—and part of me hoped that was the case, so that at least he was having a good time when the accident occurred. That was twenty years ago.

Bobby's death devastated my mother. She cried for a full week. I came home from Santa Barbara to be with my parents, but I had difficulty dealing with them. I sequestered myself in my old bedroom to avoid the accusations, the impending brawls. They began right after the funeral, and my father started drinking again, the all too familiar clink of ice in a glass each evening as he poured himself scotch after scotch. They hurled taunts at each other like poisoned darts.

"You just don't care!" she once yelled. "You've never been the father you should've been!"

"Don't point fingers at me!" He bellowed as loud as he could, as though his words could swallow up her insults, make them disappear. "You could've stayed home. Taken care of the boys. But you chose work over your own kids!"

"And how would we have lived with your paycheck?" she shot back.

"It was never about my paycheck! I know what you do at work, how you flirt with the cooks, the customers! Just like when I met you years ago."

She laughed. "At least people find me attractive, you paunchy bastard!"

I heard slaps. I heard things break. The next night, I snuck out with my suitcase, having left a note on the kitchen counter with the simple message, "Heading back to Santa Barbara. Take care." Six months later, they split up. My mom stayed in the area and within a year remarried. Her husband was a cop who early on revealed a deep resentment toward me for being the child of another man. On my visits, his eyes would bore into me as he sometimes narrowed his gaze and fix on me. Once he muttered "You think you're special, don't you?" After that, I stayed away. My dad returned to his home state of Ohio and moved in with a widowed sister. We didn't stay in touch. I don't know if he's still alive. I haven't cared enough to find out.

Most twins in my position would have wailed at the loss of their other half, fallen into a semi-permanent funk, and withdrawn from the world. But Bobby and I weren't the weeping types. We'd learned from an early age to sublimate pain, to embrace thoughts of a better future. We'd inured ourselves from grief in order to cope with our parents and their mutual torture. To be sure, a profound sadness enveloped me when he died—a kind of invisible cloud that stuck to my skin and sank inward. But I learned to live with it, like a chronic illness or a constant dull ache. My husband sees it in me sometimes, when he catches me staring off into the distance or when I'm momentarily distracted from some task. Like this morning, when I was looking out at the fog. For a few seconds, I thought I could see Bobby emerging from the mist, as though he were coming for a visit, to check up on me and see how I was doing. He was smiling the way he had for his graduation photo. I'd reached up and placed my hand on the chilly windowpane. But the image vanished.

I set Bobby's photo back on the sofa table. I looked around and took in the expanse of the living room with its soaring thirty-foot ceiling and textured walls. My husband and I were avid art collectors and we'd adorned the house with pieces we'd gathered over the years on our travels in the United States and abroad. I focused my attention on one painting we'd found in a gallery in Chicago six years prior. It was a large landscape scene by a Russian-American painter, depicting low-hill country with a few lone trees along the banks of a meandering river. Unlike many landscapes that aimed for a pretense of realism or a play with light to evoke sunsets or sunrises, what drew us was the unusual use of color. The river was a sandy brown, dull and sad, as though mud and silt flowed between its banks. There was no intent to portray shimmering water or sparkles of sunshine bouncing off a surface of sapphire and turquoise. In contrast, the sky was a brazen red, with hints of tangerine—angry, yet also inviting, as though full of passion and ready to reach out from the canvas and invite the viewer to touch its audacity. We marveled at the sight and talked about how it captured the duality of so many people—how they could be both unhappy and impassioned at the same time, how they could carry pain and yet be hopeful, how they could love and also despise. We bought it on the spot.

As I examined the painting, a sense of nostalgia washed over me. I wasn't sure where the feeling came from. I wasn't thinking about our trip to Chicago. I wasn't thinking about hanging it for the first time. I wasn't even thinking about the first painting we'd bought together—a small portrait of two smiling boys, arms draped around each other's shoulders, posed in front of the steps of a house. That piece hung upstairs in the hallway. Yet, looking at this landscape, I felt as though something in my life was missing or that maybe I'd lost something, but I couldn't determine what. My heart felt vacant, almost like it wasn't there, and for a few seconds, time stopped. Almost as soon as the sensation came, it vanished. I shook my head. Crazy.

The rustle of our cat scratching in her litter box caught my attention. I realized I hadn't seen her most of the morning. She sauntered out of the laundry room, then turned and walked into the living room.

"Hey, where ya been, Pudding?"

She ignored me as she walked past then padded up the stairs. She did favor my husband, but she'd never given me the cold shoulder before. As she disappeared at the landing, the house once again became still. I was alone, and it unsettled me.

Just then, I heard the whir of the garage door as it opened, followed by the same sound as it dropped back into place. The ADT alarm dinged to signal that someone was coming through the door. I wondered what my husband was doing home. It was only eleven o'clock. He should've been downtown at his office. He hadn't called to let me know he was coming. I turned and saw him enter. He trudged into the family room and dropped onto the sofa, burying his head in his hands. I detected a low moan and then quiet sobs. I glided through the connecting hallway and over to him.

"What's wrong, Jeffrey?"

He didn't respond.

"Honey, what's wrong?"

I caught a muffled sound coming from behind his hands. I stood there feeling helpless. I reached out for him, but he abruptly stood, then charged for the refrigerator. He pulled out a bottle of chardonnay we had opened the night before. He retrieved a glass from the cabinet and poured himself a hefty amount. He swirled the wine around just a bit, and I watched its amber color eddy within its confines, reflecting the overhead kitchen lights. Jeffrey took a large swig then drew his hand across his mouth. He looked out the window.

"Fucking fog." He spat the words out. He brought the glass to his lips once more and drained its contents. Again, he poured.

It was not like him to touch any alcohol until the workday had ended and it was time to relax. His career as an attorney had its stress and mine as an academic had its share of push and pull. So, we enjoyed our evening wind-downs with a good wine or an occasional vodka martini. But what I saw, what I'd just witnessed, was incomprehensible.

"Jeffrey, what's going on?"

He downed the entire glass and then placed it in the sink. He rested his hands on the counter and bowed his head. Once more, I heard low sobs as his body shook slightly. I waited. Over the years, I'd learned patience in our relationship, not to push him, not to engage him the way my mom and dad had engaged each other. I wasn't my parents, but I was smart enough to know how children repeat the patterns they witness, how they recreate in others what they learned early on by watching and listening. We are, after all, like cocoons with butterflies inside, waiting to emerge in an adult stage, changed from what we were when we crawled along the ground, wanting to be different, wanting to be better. Jeffrey was clearly in a state, and I needed to give him room.

He reached into his pocket and fished out his phone. He pressed a name in his contacts, then brought the phone to his ear.

"Yes. I need to speak to Tony Marshall. Tell him it's Jeffrey Lyons."

I stood there, not understanding. Tony Marshall was our financial planner. He also handled our life insurance policies.

"Tony?" Jeffrey said. His voice tottered between business and sorrow. "I...I just got back from the sheriff's office. I have some... some bad news." He continued to speak.

The words hit me with the force of the Santa Ana winds. I stumbled backwards as they echoed among my thoughts, reverberating along the canyons that had formed between memories and images. Another chill ran through me as I listened, my gaze fixed on my husband's face as tears trickled down his cheeks.

I had gone out that morning for a routine doctor's appointment in Merced. A twenty-minute drive in good weather. I should have known better, should have called and rescheduled. I'm not sure what pushed me to go. I'd made it as far as three miles on Highway 99 when a semi's taillights began to flash in the mist and the truck fishtailed then jackknifed. I made the mistake of breaking hard. The pavement was slick with fog sweat. I don't recall what happened. I just remember being home, walking into the kitchen.

Jeffrey ended the call and set his phone down on the prep island. With the back of his hand, he wiped his nose, the tears having dried up, leaving soft trails on his face. He drew in a deep breath, looked up at the ceiling, shaking his head.

"Barry, you should have stayed home," he said. "Why didn't you stay home?"

Then he hurried out of the kitchen and down the hallway, his steps thudding on the wooden stairs as he climbed to the second floor.

Quietly and slowly, I moved to the window and looked out. The fog hung like a hazy shroud. I reached up and touched my chest, hoping to feel the beat of my heart, the pulse of life. It felt as vacant as it had before, and then I understood. Out in the mist, I saw Bobby materialize and stride purposefully toward me, a broad smile across his face.

He waved, and I headed for the patio door, ready to go out and meet him.

The Night Before

Nathan rolled out of the double bed in his trailer and padded his way to the fridge on a Friday morning. He yawned, thinking how much he disliked getting up at seven, but it was the only way he could get to work in Fresno by nine. The drive there from Mañana was just over forty-five minutes when traffic cooperated. If only he could find something closer. But with limited education and no readily marketable skills, he took what he could get—a low-level office job at a company specializing in homeowner association management. He could have worked in fast food or a restaurant closer to home, but he thought such menial work was beneath him. Working in an office sounded more prestigious, even if he was making the same amount of money he might if he were serving up fried rice at Panda Express. At least his lawyer parents had bought him the trailer and the spot in the RV park so that he could have a place to call his own.

He pulled out a Diet Pepsi, popped it open, and took a sip. Like many his age, he was not a coffee drinker—he wasn't much of a drinker of anything. Since he'd turned twenty-one two years prior, he'd had at most three mixed drinks. Wine was out of the question. He despised the taste.

He rubbed at the sleep in his eyes and then looked down at the bruise on his left arm, a purplish splotch and a souvenir from the night before. It occurred to him that he should check himself in the mirror. He stepped into the bathroom area next to where he slept and switched on the light. He looked at himself, turning his head one way then another. On one side of his face, another bruise had emerged, mean and angry, along with a crimson welt. It must have been where the man's ring had caught his cheek.

He closed his eyes, images flashing like photographs being swiped past on a phone screen.

The app.

The hotel.

The man.

He opened his eyes, fished some ibuprofen from the cabinet and downed three tablets with his Pepsi. Then he made his way to the built-in sofa and plopped down. He knew he'd get questions at work, but that didn't worry him. He was a talented liar from his years of hiding who he was, he'd come up with something—and people would believe him.

* * *

He'd responded to a message he'd received on the gay dating app DikMe at eight o'clock the night before. Mostly used for hookups and not real dates, the app was always open on his iPhone. Nathan liked to stay connected. He clicked on the name of the guy who'd sent him a message. The man was exactly his type: over forty, married, and on the down low. For Nathan, such guys were perfect because they were masculine and committed to someone else, meaning no strings . Secrecy was their online currency. They also tended not to want to kiss. Nathan despised kissing. He didn't mind wrapping his mouth around some stranger's penis or having that guy penetrate him, but he abhorred the idea of lips and tongues interlocking. It was too sentimental and smacked of romance—notions he didn't understand. And because he, too, was on the down low, he didn't want to get involved with some out-and-proud gay guy who harbored desires for marriage and picket fences. Love was stupid. Monogamy was stupid. People were stupid—at least when it came to their feelings.

He checked the message. The screen name was Bad Daddy.

> Hey. What's up?

He replied and the exchange continued.

> Not much. Bored.

> Wanna play?

> Sure. Send pics.

Bad Daddy sent him photos of everything except his face. Nathan liked what he saw and sent back photos of himself, focusing on his own smooth and perfectly round butt that more than one guy had called "a sweet little ass." Nathan had learned early on how to entice such men, and Bad Daddy immediately went about setting up a meeting. An hour later, Nathan was parked in front of the local Sunrise Suites. Lots of married guys used the Sunrise for hookups, even if they lived close by. That, or they opted for car play on some unlit back road. Inviting someone to their house was out of the question. And Nathan, of course, never brought anyone to his trailer.

He went straight to the room number given to him and

knocked. The door swung open. A man about five-foot-ten stood there with full-on but neatly trimmed facial hair and a muscular body that showed through the T-shirt and jeans he sported. Nathan caught the odor of soap on the man and figured he'd just showered.

"Nathan?" the man asked.

He nodded and detected scotch on the man's breath. "Yep. And you must be Tom."

"Come on in."

He sauntered into the room and sat on the edge of the bed. Tom followed but stood in front of Nathan, the top button of his jeans open. Nathan saw the outline of his already erect penis through the denim. His own groin stirred. The man pulled off his T-shirt revealing a hairy chest and solid abs.

"Go ahead," Tom said.

Nathan reached up and undid the man's pants. Within minutes, both of them were naked and writhing on the bed.

"I need a little role play," Tom said. "You good?"

"Sure, Daddy."

Tom started. "You're a little bitch, aren't you?"

Nathan was used to how older men talked to him, especially given his five-foot-five, one-hundred-and-twenty-pound physique. He was considered a twink—a play toy for mature men. They liked that he was small, and he could play the submissive part, if needed, the "Oh, Daddy, Daddy give it to me" role. But there was a tone in this man's voice that signaled something—a low menace behind the words. Before Nathan could respond, the man backhanded him across the cheek. He felt the sting but also something else, something more than a slap. His face burned and throbbed. He realized the man's ring had bit into his face. Nathan wondered where this was headed.

"Yeah, you like it rough, don't you?"

Truth was, he didn't mind a little spanking and a little choking, but he'd never been into bondage and whipping. He'd never been struck before. He moaned a little for effect.

"Yes, Daddy."

He watched as Tom lubed himself up and then inserted his penis and began pumping. It wasn't completely unpleasurable, even though his cheek still throbbed. Then Tom hit him again—in the same spot. Pain shot across his face.

"Yeah, take it. Take it like the whore you are!"

Nathan let his mind drift, hoping it would be over soon. Then Tom climaxed. He was breathing hard. Nathan opened his eyes and watched the man roll off of him and onto his back. Nathan lay there, saying nothing. The man finally spoke.

"That was fucking awesome."

Nathan reached for his cheek. There was no blood, and a sense of relief filled him. A minute must have passed. He heard snoring, then turned to see that Tom had fallen asleep. He sat up and swung his legs over the edge of the bed, wincing through the movement, then got up. He stumbled to the bathroom and got a Kleenex to dab at his anus. He went to toss the tissue and then something told him not to. He pulled out more tissue from the dispenser and wrapped up the one in his hand. Then he snuck back into the bedroom and dressed, shoving the wad into his pocket. Tom's snoring had increased, and Nathan used the moment to rifle through the man's things until he found his wallet. There was a hundred dollars in it. He took the cash then left.

* * *

Sitting on the sofa in his trailer, Nathan looked up at the ceiling. How many times had he hooked up prior to Tom? At least once a month since he'd turned eighteen, sometimes twice a month.

He'd never encountered any violence. He decided he would block Bad Daddy on the app and never deal with him again. Filing a report was out of the question. He'd have to give DikMe information he didn't want others to know. And what if his parents found out? Would they cut him off? The image of his older brother who occasionally pried into his life with, "Are you sure you're not gay?"

He wondered why he cared about what his family thought or said. He didn't have much of a relationship with them. He was the failure, the child who was less than average in school, the one who would never go to college, who had to listen to his condescending father after his older brother graduated from UC Merced.

"Not everyone is meant for higher education, son."

He'd disconnected his emotional strings to them years before and learned to take from them what he could get. Money. Clothes. The trailer. He played the role of the grateful son as best he could, when internally he felt nothing for his parents or his brother. They were just people, as stupid as everyone else.

After he showered and dressed, he headed down Highway 99 toward Fresno. About five miles south of Madera, he saw flashing lights behind him.

"Shit," he muttered.

He had been doing ninety and usually no cops ever paid attention. He slowed and pulled over to the shoulder, checking the clock on his dash. Fuck. He'd probably be late for work now. He could see the highway patrolman exit his vehicle and come around the passenger side. Nathan lowered the window. A semi sped by, and his car shook from the tremor.

"You were going pretty fast there," the man said, removing his sunglasses.

And then Nathan recognized him. Tom. He must have done the same as his brow arched when he took a good look at Nathan.

"Well, well," he said. "Look who we have here."

"Hi, Tom."

There was an awkward silence. Then Tom said, "You snuck away last night."

Nathan shrugged. "You were snoring."

Tom spat on the ground. "You wouldn't happen to know where my hundred dollars are, would you?"

His face was placid, in the way cops were trained to not show emotion, but Nathan detected the same low level of menace he'd heard in the man's voice the night before. For a second, he wondered what would happen. Then he remembered that this highway patrol cop was a married man on the down low. He had a secret, and Nathan had the tissue. He pulled one side of his mouth up into a smirk.

"Why don't you ask your wife?" he said. He looked at the name embroidered on the man's left chest. "Officer Henley, is it?"

Tom's face slackened into a frown. He looked away and then back at Nathan. There was another awkward pause.

"Well, how about I let you go this one time? But remember. I have your license plate."

"And I know who you are," Nathan said.

They stared at each other—gazes locked like gunfighters in an old western movie, hands hovering over pistols. Finally, Tom patted the passenger door.

"Okay, then. You can go."

Firing his last salvo, Nathan said, "Thank you, Officer Henley. Give my regards to the family."

He raised the passenger window, drew in a deep breath, and started his car. He pulled back out onto the highway and watched in his rearview mirror as the man ambled back to his vehicle and got in. Within minutes, Nathan had left him far behind.

* * *

Nathan swept into the management office and headed for his cubicle. Sherri, another worker, stopped him.

"Hey, what happened to you?" she said, eyeing his face.

"Clumsy me," he replied, grinning. "Yesterday I was coming out of my trailer while talking on my phone. I missed a step and boom! Face and ground became one."

Sherri chuckled and flapped her hand in the air. "We've all been there. I fractured my foot one year just getting out of bed. Silly, right?"

He chuckled in return. She bustled off, and he settled into his cubicle then fired up his computer. Yes, lying was easy. Most people would believe anything if you said it right. Probably like Officer Tom Henley's wife.

He reached into his shoulder bag and pulled out the wad of tissue from the night before. He'd secured it in a baggie when he'd gotten home. He looked at it, put it away, and then smiled.

Yes, I know who you are. And he thought about how one-hundred dollars wasn't much money. His silence was worth much more, wasn't it?

Buzz

The mid-June sun beat down without mercy as eleven-year-old Sarah Tucker sat cross-legged near the railroad tracks in Mañana. In 1951, there wasn't much to do in a town of just under four-thousand souls, and Sarah had taken to counting railroad cars each time a train would pass. She knew the schedule by heart and would set out about a half-hour before each passing, grab her spot, and read her book—a memoir by Amelia Earhart, *The Fun of It*—as she waited. Then she would set her book to the side when she heard the train's approach. The first few times she just counted out loud but then she got it in her head to keep a record, so she logged each train into a journal with the date, time, and number of cars that trailed behind the engine. On this day, she counted forty-four as the long line rushed by, the breeze from its push like invisible fingers twirling her hair.

"That was a long one," she said as she penciled in the information.

After the caboose had clickety-clacked away, she opened her book and read a few more pages. Earhart had defied all odds in a career that only men were supposed to follow. Sarah's gaze focused on a sentence.

> *Usually it is not until girls reach college that any comparative attention is paid to them.*

Amelia had been talking about sports and physical fitness. Sarah pondered this observation, thinking about how her older brother, Billy, had been trained in athletics since he was ten, and now he was a high school baseball phenom. Her own mother seemed to be confined to the house and the only physical activity she engaged in revolved around cleaning, doing laundry, and cooking. Sarah had once asked her if she ever played any sports.

"Girls don't do that sort of thing," her mother had replied.

Sitting by the railroad tracks and reading about Amelia Earhart's adventures, Sarah decided she would not be a typical girl. She wanted to fly planes just like her heroine. She would visit new places, see the world, get away from the town she lived in where tractors and combines crawled along the farmlands kicking up dust and obscuring her view of the distant Sierras. There had to be more to life than the fields of cotton, hay, and barley that dominated the flat landscape of the San Joaquin Valley. Europe. Australia. Africa. These were all places she dreamed of, flying in low to land at an airport, and then stepping out of the plane and into some new adventure, greeted by locals and eating something other than meat, potatoes, and green vegetables.

Maybe she could cajole her brother into teaching her how to wield a bat and pitch a ball. He could train her, coach her. She needed to be physically fit if she was going to be like Amelia.

A buzz sounded from above, and Sarah shielded her eyes as she looked up. A crop duster was on an errand, and she followed its path until it disappeared from view. The only sound remaining was the caw of a crow that had landed on the skeletal limb of a leafless tree about ten yards away. *Maybe I could learn crop dusting*, she thought. *That would get me started, wouldn't it?*

She picked herself up off the ground and brushed off her dungarees. Her mom would scold her if she came home sullied. She plodded over to where her bicycle lay, pulled it upright and set her book and journal inside the basket, then placed a heavy rock on them so they wouldn't blow away. She hopped on and set out on the three-mile ride home.

On the way, she stopped at the town's only gas station—a two pump affair with a big Texaco star on the roof—to buy a Coke with the nickel her dad had given her that morning before he'd left for work on a local farm. She shoved the coin into the bright red machine and then pulled open the side door to retrieve a bottle from its locked position. Just then, Tommy emerged from inside—a forty-something-year-old man who people sometimes talked about because he'd never married and lived alone. Sarah didn't understand the word "queer" when she heard it, she only understood that it meant Tommy was bad somehow—and Billy would not explain the word to her. What she did know from her own experience was that Tommy had kind eyes and was the only person who spoke to her as he would to other adults. He'd been working at the gas station for as long as she could remember, so he must be good at his job. He was also a dog lover and had rescued two abandoned pups along the road. He named them "Ricky" and "Teddy", after two friends he'd met in the army and who'd died in battle. What could be so bad about someone like him?

"Hey there, Sarah. Out counting trains again?"

"Yeah. And reading."

He was the only one who knew about her self-appointed task of train watching and he never made light of it. In fact, one time he'd told her about a summer as a teenager when he'd hopped a freight car just to see where it would take him.

"I wound up in Stockton," he said. "Had to wait half a day for a train to come back the other way so I could get home."

Stockton was ninety miles up the road but for Sarah it might as well have been 9,000. She never got out of Mañana. Their relatives all lived within a twenty-mile radius and their homes were the only places she got to visit, usually for post-church Sunday dinner. The farthest she'd ever been was Los Banos when she was six years old, and that was to accompany her dad and brother to get him enrolled in a summer baseball camp.

"Why Amelia Earhart?" Tommy asked as he jutted his chin at the book.

She sipped on her Coke and wiped her mouth with the back of her hand. "I want to be like her."

"You want to be a pilot?"

"Sure. Why not?"

"Well," he said, as he dropped his own nickel into the Coke machine, "I think that's a great idea. You know, I have a friend who works out at the airstrip. Maybe your parents would let me take you out to meet him."

Her eyes widened. "Really?"

He pried off the bottle cap on the machine's opener and took a swig. "Heck yeah. He's got a daughter about your age. She goes with him to work sometimes."

Sarah felt the pangs of envy. She would do anything to be able to hang out at an airstrip, watch the planes, maybe even sit in one. The mere thought of being in the cockpit, touching the controls, seeing it all up close, sent a tingle throughout her body. Just then, the overhead bell dinged as a car pulled in.

"Duty calls," he said. But as he walked away to wait on the customer, he spun around. "I'll ask my friend. See what he says. Come back and see me."

"You bet!" she called out.

She downed her Coke, put the empty bottle in the machine's side container, and then hopped on her bike. As she pedaled, she smiled with the buoyancy of anticipation that she would get to visit the airstrip with Tommy in the near future. Slowly, she extended her arms out to the side, riding without hands, transforming herself into a human airplane. She imagined she was on a runway getting ready to take off.

"I'm Amelia Earhart!" she cried.

Then she brought her arms back in and took control of the handlebars once more, giggling. When she got home, she parked her bike on the side of the house and found her mother bringing clothes in off the line.

"It's about time!" she said. "Young lady, I've been waiting for you to get home and help me with this!"

Sarah bustled over, still elated.

"Mom, guess what," she said, almost out of breath. "I saw Tommy at the gas station, and he said he knows someone at the airstrip."

She grabbed one of the side handles of the wicker laundry basket while her mother grabbed the other.

"So?" Her mother kept her gaze fixed on the steps leading to the back door.

"He said he could take me, and I could see the planes and talk to people there!"

"And why would you want to do that?"

"Mom! Amelia Earhart! I'm reading about her. I want to fly planes!"

They paused at the house and her mom set her side of the basket down on the steps as she reached for the back-door screen.

"Sarah Marie Tucker. I don't know where you get these ideas. Women aren't pilots. And look what happened to that Amelia Air Heart anyway. Dead somewhere in the ocean. Now go put your bike away and then come help me fold these clothes."

She grabbed the basket but before entering the house, she turned to her daughter.

"And be careful of that Tommy. He's a strange one."

"He is not!" Sarah knew better than to contradict her mother, but the words came out before she could stop herself. "He's really nice and he even said the man at the airstrip takes his own daughter there sometimes."

Her mom clucked her tongue and shook her head, then entered the house. Sarah trudged over to her bike and walked it to the garage, her lower lip jutting out, as curse words formed in her head that she didn't dare let erupt from her mouth. She'd just talked back to her mother, and she knew she'd hear about it at dinner from her dad. She retrieved her book and journal from the basket and leaned up against the wall. Flies buzzed overhead, and she closed her eyes, trying to imagine them as propellered planes on their way to some exotic destination.

After dinner, Sarah dried and put away the dishes. The sun had just dipped below the horizon as night crept in. The evening sound of chirping crickets filtered through the kitchen window. Billy sat at the dining room table doing homework. Her dad sat in in the living room next to where the radio was perched, the nightly news crackling from its speakers, his face buried in the newspaper. Her mom crocheted. Sarah had joined them, sitting on the floor with legs crossed, reading. A knock at the door interrupted the family's evening routine.

"Who could that be?" her father asked as he lowered the volume of the radio.

She watched as her brother scooted back the dining room chair and got up to answer the door.

"Hi. Is Sarah here?"

It was Tommy. What was he doing there? Her dad rose from his chair and approached.

"Hello, Tommy."

"Good evening, Mr. Tucker."

Sarah jumped up and hurried next to her dad, the glow of her mother's side lamp seeping into the foyer of their turn-of-the century farmhouse. She grinned.

"Hi, Tommy!"

They seldom received visitors and she had a hunch Tommy was there because of their earlier conversation. He stood there, holding his ball cap in his hands. He must have gone home and cleaned up, because he was dressed in jeans and a short sleeve buttoned up shirt, not in his gas station dungarees. His hands had been scrubbed of grease and oil. She wondered why her dad hadn't invited him to come in and sit down.

"What can we do for you?" her father said.

"Well, I came to tell Sarah that I spoke to my friend at the airstrip." He turned to her. "It's all set up. You can visit this weekend, if it's alright with your parents." He looked up at Mr. Tucker.

Sarah clapped her hands. "Wow! That's great!"

"Hold on a minute," her dad said, placing his hand on her shoulder. "Sarah told us what this is about. Her mother and I are not sure this is a good idea."

Sarah looked up at her dad. What was he saying? She turned toward her mother, still crocheting under the light of her chairside lamp and seemingly ignoring the men's conversation. But Sarah was positive she wasn't missing a word. When had she and her dad talked, and why hadn't they spoken with her?

"If you're concerned about safety, you needn't be," Tommy said. "And, of course, you would come with Sarah. It would only be for a short time. Maybe an hour or so."

Sarah tugged on her father's hand. "Please, Dad! This is a dream come true!"

Her dad looked down at her, pursing his lips. He cast a glance at her mom then returned his attention to Sarah. She pleaded with her eyes.

"I appreciate your coming," he said as he redirected his attention to Tommy. "We're just not comfortable with the situation."

Wait, Sarah thought. *Is this because of Tommy?* There were rumors about him, that he was odd, or queer in some way. But she only knew him to be a good guy, the friendly man at the gas pump who always greeted her with a smile.

"Dad," she said. "You could take me. And Billy could come to." She looked at her brother, who stood to the left and slightly behind her dad. "You like planes, don' you?"

"Sure," he said. Then he bowed his head and Sarah understood that he realized he'd spoken when he shouldn't have.

"Sarah, that's enough," her dad said. "You too, Billy." He looked at Tommy standing in front of him. "Thank you for stopping by."

Tommy took one last look at Sarah, smiled slightly, and then nodded at her father. He placed his ballcap on his head and turned. Her dad closed the door gently behind him. Within minutes, the family had settled back into its evening routine—her dad listening to news on the radio, her mom's fingers nimbly moving the crochet hook and yarn, and her brother doing homework at the dining table. Sarah swallowed her disappointment by biting on her lower lip, then sat on a chair with her book. She turned to a page with a photograph of Amelia Earhart standing at the side of a plane, one foot on the wheel cover, hand on one hip. She smiled broadly at the camera and the caption said, "My solo flight across the Atlantic was on this Lockheed Vega 5B. This is my 'Little Red Bus.'" Sarah thought it was fun to have a nickname for a plane. She closed her eyes and imagined what it would have been like to sit in the cockpit and take off for Europe.

If only, she thought.

The next day, Sarah left the train tracks after her usual counting of cars. She stopped at the Texaco station and Tommy came out to greet her.

"Hello, Sarah."

"Hi, Tommy." She paused, remembering what had happened the night before. "Thanks for coming by."

He repositioned the ballcap on his sweaty head. "You and your parents talk? They gonna let you go this weekend?"

She shrugged. "I don't know. Maybe we'll talk today. I just wanted to say thanks."

"My pleasure," he said.

She said goodbye and hopped on her bike. She never made it to the airstrip that weekend. In fact, she never saw Tommy again. A day later, her parents spoke after dinner while seated in the living room. She sat on the last step of the staircase, her Amelia Earhart book open on her lap.

"I suppose you heard about Tommy," her dad said.

Sarah's ears pricked up and she turned her attention to the living room.

"Mary Ann told me this afternoon." Her mom had not lifted her gaze from the sewing chore in her hands. Mary Ann was a chicken-rearing neighbor down the road, someone well connected to the grapevine in the small town of Mañana, who spent as much time clucking gossip as collecting eggs. Sarah found her both amusing and annoying.

"He probably had it coming."

"Probably," her mother added.

Her dad switched on the radio and tuned it to the news.

Sarah wanted to ask what happened, what they were talking about. But she'd learned early on as a child not to ask questions during an adult conversation. If they'd wanted her to know anything, they would have called her over. She went to bed that night, her mind a jumble of questions about Tommy and what exactly he'd had coming to him. Her brother had been no help when she asked what he knew.

"Best you don't know," he said.

Worry settled on her, and she lay in bed clutching her pillow. Something bad must have happened to Tommy, but what? Finally, sometime after midnight, she drifted into sleep. During the night, fleeting images of her friend appeared in dreams about the airstrip.

The next morning, she beelined for the Texaco station. She leaned her bike up against the Coke machine and then hurried to the door. She expected to see her friend appear and greet her with a smile as he always did. But instead, Sam, the evening shift attendant, emerged from the garage bay and saw her. He waved. She scrunched up her face, wondering why he was there.

"I guess you heard about Tommy," Sam said.

"No. Where is he?"

He spat onto the greasy pavement. "I suppose at Weldon's Memorial Chapel." He pulled a handkerchief from his back pocket and mopped his brow. "They found him dead by his car out on Avenue 28, by the reservoir."

Sarah's eyes went wide. "He—he died?"

"Yep. From the looks of it, he took one hell of a beating. Maybe from a baseball bat. I heard one side of his head was pretty bad." He shook his head. "I knew something like this would happen to him."

Before Sarah could ask him what he meant, a car pulled in and tripped the overhead bell. Sam waltzed over to attend to the customer. Sarah stood there, rigid. Tommy, her friend, the man who promised to take her to the airstrip, the attendant she drank Cokes with, had been killed—beaten to death from what Sam had just said. Who would do that to a nice guy like him? Why wouldn't her parents have told her? An unknown feeling gathered in her stomach and pushed its way upward. Tears formed in her eyes. She brushed at them with the back of her hand. Slowly, she turned and trudged to her bike, hopped on, and headed for the railroad tracks.

Fifteen minutes later, she was seated in her usual spot, but this day she didn't count cars. She sat there, knees pulled up to her chest, throwing pebbles at the steel rail thirty feet away and thinking about Tommy. He'd come to her house and asked her parents in person if she could go to the airstrip with him. Why had her parents been so reluctant? What was it about Tommy that they didn't like? Why did her mother tell her to be careful, that he was an odd one? What did her brother know? And now Tommy was dead. Something just wasn't right, and no one would tell her.

She folded her arms on her knees and rested her head. The tears flowed as the local crop duster buzzed overhead. She looked up, squinting with red-rimmed eyes.

"Someday, Tommy," she said. "I will be a pilot."

Dark

When Patricia Buckbee's son Eric brought his new girlfriend for a visit, she smiled politely in a not so successful attempt to hide her surprise. He'd mentioned her on a number of occasions, having dated her for almost a year. But for some reason, the two had never made it down to Mañana from Sacramento. Patricia was eager to meet her son's new love interest given his enthusiasm when he talked about her.

"I think I'm going to do it again," he'd once said in a phone call.

Do it again referred to a second marriage, his first one ending in divorce some five years before. He'd had no children from that union, and Patricia was anxious to be a grandmother. In her circle of retired friends, she was the only woman who didn't have photos of grandchildren to share at lunches. When Eric announced he was once again contemplating marriage, she swelled with hope at the thought that maybe in a year or so, she'd be able to dote on a new baby in the family.

"But I think we should live together for a while," he added. "Make sure it's right."

Eric's pronouncement had settled on her like a crown of

thorns. Born and raised in Mañana and never having traveled out of state in her sixty-eight-year existence, Patricia was a traditionalist. Her parents were from Mañana, and their parents as well, and her husband claimed even one more generation before that. Between the two of them, family roots ran deep in this part of the Central Valley—deeper than those of the thousands of acres of almond trees. What if Eric had a child before tying the knot? Even though her son lived two hours north off Highway 99, news like that couldn't be kept from the folks in Mañana. She imagined the tongues clucking at the local Church of the Resurrection.

So, when her son walked in that day with his girlfriend, Kerry Davis, Patricia's pulse ticked up as she suppressed a swallow. Kerry was five-feet-four, slim, attractive—and had skin the color of coffee with a dab of cream. *Oh no*, Patricia thought. *Why didn't he tell us?* Kerry reached out to shake Patricia's hand.

"It's such a pleasure to meet you, Mrs. Buckbee. Eric speaks of his family often."

Patricia offered a light, uncommitted grip. "Well, it's good to finally meet you."

She ushered Eric and Kerry into the great room.

"You have a lovely home," Kerry said.

"Thank you," Patricia said as she gestured for them to take a seat.

She wasn't sure if Kerry meant what she'd said or was just being polite. In the end, what difference did it make? She had to worry about her husband in the event he came home while their son and his girlfriend were there. She excused herself and hurried over to the kitchen to fetch the coffee and cookies she'd prepared earlier. Out of their line of sight, she clasped her hands and offered a silent prayer. *Oh, Lord. What is my son doing? Please don't let Richard come home right now.* Once she'd composed herself, she carried a tray out to her guests and set it down on the cocktail table, then poured three cups and invited Kerry to help herself to the treats.

"Is dad around?" Eric asked, his brow wrinkled from worry.

"He's out golfing." She cleared her throat as she turned to Kerry. "Ever since he retired, my husband has become a golf fanatic. So, Kerry, are you from Sacramento?"

Kerry set her coffee cup down. "No. My family moved to California from Missouri when I was ten. My dad is ex-military and my mother just recently retired. She was a paralegal."

"Oh, that's nice." Patricia sipped on her coffee, hoping that the slight tremble in her hand wasn't visible. She cleared her throat once more. "We were hoping Eric would stay in the area, maybe even buy a home here in The Palms. But he drifted away."

The Palms was a gated community in Mañana. Wrapped around a golf course, The Palms consisted of hundreds of homes with private parks, a club house, and twenty-four-hour security. Patricia and her husband had moved there twelve years before, selling their country home four miles away. Like most folks from the area, they'd considered the move a step up and a way to distance themselves from the increasing riff raff in the neighborhoods on the other side of Highway 99.

"I had to go where my work took me, Mom." He reached for a cookie.

Patricia knew better. Eric had always felt out of place in Mañana, telling her once that the town was just too small for him. At first, she took his comment as a slight. The town was good enough for her but not for him. But as she prayed on it, she realized that children grow up and leave the nest, sometimes flying further away than their parents wanted.

"So, your father's ex-military?" Patricia said to Kerry.

"Yes. He worked in intelligence for twenty years before moving into the private sector." Kerry picked up her cup and sipped.

"And what does he do now?"

Kerry dabbed her mouth with a napkin. "He's recently retired but he was an IT manager for supermarkets. The chain owned by SaveMart." She glanced around. "May I use the restroom?"

"Of course." Patricia directed her to the hallway. "The first door on your right."

Kelly stood and left the room. Patricia fixed her gaze on her son.

"Why didn't you tell us? You know how your father is going to react."

Eric leaned back into the sofa. "Mom, I'm forty years old. I don't need to tell you anything and, besides, Dad needs to deal with it. So do you."

"And so what? You think you can just waltz in here like this? Spring this on us?"

"You know damned well if I'd said anything over the phone that you would have told me not to bring her by, that you didn't want to meet her." He leaned forward. "This way, you can see what a great person she is. Judge her for that." He paused. "We talked, you know. I told her what to expect. And yet, here she is, unafraid of the firing squad."

Patricia's jaw dropped at such an image, but before she could say anything, Kelly re-entered the room. Patricia composed herself, contemplating where to take the conversation. In one of his phone calls, Eric had said Kerry was a dental hygienist in Sacramento, where he'd met her. Patricia was on the verge of asking about Kerry's own career when her son spoke.

"Mom. We have something to tell you."

Patricia's gaze fell on a diamond ring sparkling from the girl's left hand. She hadn't noticed it earlier, shocked by Kelly's skin color and distracted by her son's audacity at bringing her to the house. That ring meant only one thing. Her stomach tightened and she quickly looked down at her coffee. Just then, the whir of the garage door signaled that her husband had returned. She briefly shut her eyes. *The strength, please! The strength!* She stood.

"Hold on, Honey," she said to her son. "I think I hear your dad coming."

She hustled to the laundry room and opened the door that led to the garage. She reached her husband just as he was stepping out of the car. Not a tall man, Richard Buckbee had the look of someone who'd lived a lot of his life outdoors. Lines carved his face like the furrows of the fields he once tilled in his teenage years, and his faded blue eyes had long ago lost the spark of youthful exuberance.

"Richie, Eric is here."

"I know. I saw his car."

"He brought his girlfriend with him."

"Oh. He did?"

She bit her lip. "There's something you need to know before you go in."

He raised the eyebrows on his perpetually frowned face.

"She's…she's dark."

Dark. That was the word they used instead of African American or even black. It was a term they'd learned from their parents, who had learned it from their parents. He squinted at her.

"You mean…"

She nodded vigorously. He looked toward the door that led into the house then back at her.

"You're kidding me?"

She shook her head.

"And he didn't tell us?"

Patricia refrained from telling him about her conversation with Eric a few minutes before. She reached out to her husband, placing her hands on his upper arms.

"I don't want a scene."

He eyed her, like he was contemplating the situation. "They could get married. Have children. They'd be…"

"Richie, now listen."

The door from the laundry room opened and Eric appeared. "Hello, Dad."

Richard brushed past his wife and stepped toward his son and stood two feet from him. He locked his gaze on Eric.

"Your mother tells me you brought a darkie home. Why didn't you tell us?"

Eric leaned in slightly. "Because in my mind, it isn't an issue."

"It is to me! And to your mother! You knew this and you didn't say anything!"

Patricia recognized her husband's tone—the brick wall tone, the tone that defied anyone to say something different, the tone he'd used on Eric the teenager to ensure he turned into a real man.

"Dad, you have got to get over this hatred of yours." Eric's voice rose, almost to the level of a shout. "I love Kerry just as you love Mom! Color should make no difference!"

By this time, Patricia's husband's face had turned the color of hot lava. "Bullshit! I won't have it! No grandchildren of mine are going to have mixed blood!"

Eric narrowed his eyes. Patricia worried about what he might say and wondered if their elevated voices had carried into the living room. She raised her hand to her mouth as she bit into a loose fist.

"Mom," Eric said, "are you going to say anything?"

She stayed silent. Her years with Richard had trained her to acquiescence when confrontation loomed. She'd let this play out between the two men.

"So be it," her son said, almost spitting out the words. "You won't ever see me again."

He spun on his heel, then abruptly stopped.

"And getting married isn't the news we had for you," he said. "I'm going to be a father."

Patricia's eyes went wide. She took a step, but her son turned and pushed through the door leading into the laundry area before she could say anything. She closed her eyes and bowed her head. Her husband mumbled something. She looked up at him and then heard the front door open and close, followed by the sound of Eric's car starting up and pulling away. Richard turned to her.

"Not in my home," he said.

He left Patricia standing there as he stormed into the house. She brushed away a tear and then clasped her hands.

"Dear Lord," she said. "Help me through this. Help me do the right thing for my family."

In her heart, she already knew what the right thing was. The question was whether she had the strength to do it.

* * *

The months came and went, slowly it seemed to Patricia. Eric never called, but she tried to reach him a number of times, only to get his voicemail. Her messages were the same. *Honey. I miss you. I'm so sorry. Please call me.* She'd consulted with her pastor, whose only advice was to seek the Lord's guidance through prayer.

"But he's not answering me," she said.

The exasperation in her voice was clear. The pastor reached for her hands and clasped them gently in his own.

"What do you want to do?" he asked.

"I want to see my son. And, I guess, well, I want to be there when his child is born."

"Then," he said, "the Lord *has* spoken to you."

On a Friday morning, Patricia's phone chirped, the caller ID displaying her son's name. Her heart rate ticked up.

"Hi, Eric." She couldn't contain the joy in her voice.

"I'm at Kaiser Hospital," he said. "Kerry's in labor. I'm going in to be with her. I thought I'd let you know."

He hung up, leaving Patricia with the phone still by her ear. She sat, staring at nothing, a single thought in her mind. *I'm having a grandchild and I don't even know if it's a boy or a girl.* Richard was down in Madera at the Home Depot and would return to play golf with two buddies. Without much internal debate, she jumped up, grabbed her purse and keys, and hustled to her car. She sped down Highway 99 and made it to Sacramento in just under two hours. She knew where the hospital was, having visited Eric there two years before after he'd had emergency surgery for a hernia. She parked and rushed inside. A young woman sat at an information desk. Patricia ran up to her.

"My daughter-in-law is having a baby. Where is maternity?"

The young woman gave her directions and she hurried to the elevator, her low pumps clicking on the slick floor. The doors opened on the third level, and she bustled to the nurses' station. Just then, Eric appeared from a doorway, dressed in scrubs and a cap, a surgical mask dangling from one ear.

"Mom?" he said, his head tilted in surprise.

She rushed over to him. "I just had to come! How is she?"

"I'm not sure. There seems to be complications. The doctor told me to come out for some air."

"Complications? What kind of complications?"

Before he could answer, a nurse appeared.

"Mr. Buckbee, the doctor thinks you should come back in now."

Eric looked at his mother, and she could see the worry behind his brown eyes. She hugged him and told him to go.

"I'll wait out here," she said.

Patricia sat, wringing her hands and watching hospital personnel come and go at the nurses' station. She looked at her watch several times. *What was happening?* Finally, a nurse emerged from the delivery room and approached her.

"Mrs. Buckbee?"

Patricia stood. "Yes?"

"Your son asked me to come out and talk to you."

"Why? What's wrong?"

"Let's sit down."

"No, please. Just tell me."

"The baby is fine. She's a healthy little girl."

A granddaughter! Patricia wondered what they'd named her. Probably after someone in Kerry's family. That would make sense. The nurse continued.

"Mrs. Buckbee—Kerry, I mean—hemorrhaged considerably."

Patricia brought her hand to her mouth as she gasped.

"We did the best we could. She died a few minutes ago. Your son is still with her. I'm so sorry."

Patricia sunk onto the chair, her lips trembling.

"Are you okay, Mrs. Buckbee?" the nurse asked.

She looked up. "Oh, yes. I'm just, well, shocked."

"You and your daughter-in-law must have been close."

Patricia said nothing, avoiding eye contact.

"I'll leave you to your thoughts," the nurse said. "But if you need anything, just check with the receptionist."

Patricia nodded and the nurse disappeared. Alone once again, she cast her eyes down, staring at the reflection of the overhead fluorescent lights on the linoleum floor. For some time, she remained silent, her focus unchanged, her stomach churning from a mix of remorse and guilt. *I let him down*, she thought. *I let my son down.* Damn! She'd been so worried about the gossips in Mañana that she'd turned her back on her only child.

She'd let her husband dictate her behavior, even though it went against what she felt in her heart. She prayed silently. *Lord, forgive me. The commandment is to honor thy mother and father, but what about honoring our children? My son needed me. How can I call myself a good mother?*

She felt a presence and looked up to see Eric taking the seat next to her. His eyes were red, spider-veined from tears that had dried up on his cheeks. She reached for his hand.

"I'm so, so sorry."

He pinched the bridge of his nose, and she placed one hand on his shoulder as he choked back the sobs.

"I held her hand, Mom. I held her hand while she died."

Her eyes glistened as she read the pain in her son's face.

"What am I going to do?" he said.

She pulled him into her bosom as she had done so many times when he was a child—after a bike fall, after a knee scrape, after a bee sting. But this was no bee sting, and she clung to him as she rocked him slightly, cooing into his ear.

"I'm here, Baby. I'm here."

Some twenty minutes must've passed before Eric composed himself. He brushed at his face with the back of his hand as he pulled back.

"Thank you, Mom."

She smiled. "I've been such a fool. Do you forgive me?"

"I love you," he said. "I always will."

Her heard fluttered. *I raised a great son,* she thought.

"Would you…would you like to see her?" he asked.

"The baby?"

He nodded, still wiping his eyes.

"Oh, Honey! Yes! I would!"

They stood, wrapped their arms around each other's waists, and headed down the hallway. As they made their way to the nursery, Patricia knew then what she had to do—and Richard wouldn't like it.

But she didn't care.

Dawn

As ten-year-old Dawn entered the Goodwill drop-off station in Madera, she dragged a garbage bag full of clothes behind her. She huffed and puffed as she made the haul. It didn't help that the temperature was about to hit ninety degrees on this day in early June or the smoke from a wildfire near Mariposa had drifted down into the Central Valley.

"This weighs a ton!" she cried with exasperation.

"Well, you wanted to do it by yourself," her mother replied.

She offered a smile that was really an *I-told-you-so*. Moms knew how to do that look really well. Dawn ignored it.

"I should have put this on my wagon."

"But you gave that away last week," her mother added, still smiling.

"Well, that was a mistake," Dawn said.

She stopped and blew the bangs away from her face, then crinkled her nose at the smell of Lysol filling the room. A woman was spraying down the counter and wiping it clean, pulling her face into a pinched look that meant only one thing: *Yuck*. Dawn brushed away the idea of the place being filled with the germs carried in on unwanted items. Her mom had made sure all the clothes in her bag were clean before they brought them in, and Dawn felt a sense of satisfaction at not bringing in unsanitary items.

She was there to make a donation, the idea of charity and do-unto-others instilled in her since she could talk. One of the earliest books her mother had shared with her was *The Bernstein Bears Think of Those in Need*. And once Dawn had turned eight, her mother had taught her that for every dollar she earned in allowance, she should put aside ten cents for charity. Just recently, she'd donated a whole twenty dollars to the local Ronald Mac-Donald House in Fresno. She knew it wasn't a big amount, but as her mother had said, if one million people each gave twenty dollars, that would be twenty million.

That morning, as she pondered what to do with the clothes she no longer needed, it occurred to her they could be used by a kid who maybe couldn't afford to buy new. So, off they went to the Goodwill. Struggling with the garbage bag, Dawn realized it really wasn't that much of a burden. If Jesus Christ could carry his cross, she could certainly handle this one task.

She finally made it to a table where a plump lady with salt-and-pepper hair waited to receive the donation. She looked to be around the same age as Dawn's grandmother, but there wasn't any resemblance beyond that. Her nana wore glasses, used bright red lipstick, and smelled of rose water. Plus, she went to the salon once a week to get her hair done. She didn't dye it, saying she didn't see the need for that, but she did like her silver locks to be styled regularly.

"Always look smart when you go out in public," she'd told Dawn.

In contrast, the Goodwill lady sported faded jeans and a T-shirt from the Chukchansi Casino. Her flat hair was scooped behind her ears, and she smelled of a breakfast burrito she must have just eaten. Dawn thought the woman fit right in as she glanced around the drop-off center. Makeshift tables, piles of donations in the corner that weren't clothes, a dingy linoleum floor. She lived with her mom in a nice home in Mañana, where everything was scrubbed clean and the house always smelled of scented candles. Vanilla usually. She shifted her attention to the reason she was there, and dusted off her hands, then placed them on her hips.

"I'm giving away my old clothes," she said, as the woman hoisted the bag onto the table. "I don't need them anymore."

"Well, that's very generous of you," the woman said. "Let's see what you have here."

She opened the bag and turned its contents out onto the table, poised to push the items into the large bin where donated clothes wound up for processing. She pulled shirts and pants out and held some up for a quick inspection, her brow furrowing after examining four of them.

"These are boys' clothes."

"Yes."

Dawn's tone was matter of fact, the same she might use to tell her mom she needed new pencils for school or that the mail had arrived. The woman looked behind Dawn, as though searching for someone.

"Are these your brother's" she asked.

"No."

"Well, they're not yours."

"Not anymore," Dawn answered. She was slightly annoyed at the woman. Dawn was there to make a donation, and she'd already told the woman they were her old clothes. Besides, why the concern for who the clothes belonged to?

"I get it," the woman said. "My daughter was a tomboy, too. She preferred boys' clothes until she got to the third grade. I guess that's what happened to you."

Dawn contemplated what to say. She could disregard the woman, or she could speak her truth, to borrow a phrase from her mother. She remembered the first time she had. Two months before, she'd waltzed into class dressed in an Old Navy tulip-sleeved hem-long pink top with purple and rose-colored leggings. Her mother had offered to call and speak with the school before Dawn showed up, but Dawn insisted she not do that.

"Are you sure?" her mom asked.

"Yep. Gotta fend for myself."

When her teacher laid eyes on her, she said, "Donald, why are you dressed like that?"

"My name isn't Donald. It's Dawn. Like the sunrise."

Her teacher scrunched her face. Dawn just looked at her. Her mother had said people might need some time to adjust and for her to be prepared. Several seconds ticked off before the teacher's eyes widened.

"Oh," she said, nodding. "I understand."

Would the Goodwill woman understand? Dawn wasn't sure, so she decided to explain. "I'm a girl now. Well, actually, I always was a girl. I just got the wrong body. So, that's why I don't need these clothes."

The woman's face flushed. She looked at Dawn's mother and then back at Dawn.

"I'm, uh, well, I guess…I guess you don't need these." She began pulling clothes out of the bag and then stopped midway. She looked up at Dawn's mother. "Are you sure you know what you're doing?"

Dawn turned to see her mom take a step forward. She signaled her mother to stop.

"That's okay," she said. "I can do this." She took in a deep breath, then turned to face the woman again. She paused as she tilted her head. "Have you ever felt like you were someone else?"

The Goodwill woman froze. "Well, I, uh, no. Not really."

Dawn crossed her arms. "So, there's nothing about you that you know is out of sync?" 'Out of sync' was a term her mom had used when Dawn first declared she was a girl. Bodies and minds or hearts could be out of sync.

The woman looked at Dawn's mother again. But her mom said nothing. She'd told Dawn that she was precocious—a word that Dawn had come to savor as much for its three-syllable sound as its meaning. Her mother had added that adults might struggle with her forthrightness, and she'd need to be strong. And here was one instance. The Goodwill woman looked back at Dawn.

"How old are you?"

"Ten."

"Well, don't you think a ten-year-old shouldn't ask adults questions like the one you just asked me?"

"Just because I'm a kid doesn't mean I can't ask questions." Dawn squinted slightly. "Does it make you feel uncomfortable?"

The woman looked away for a moment. "Not really."

Dawn could tell that wasn't true.

"And how do you know for sure you want to be a girl?" the woman asked.

"I don't *want* to be girl," Dawn replied, her voice ticking up slightly. "I *am* a girl."

The woman grunted. "God made you a boy and you'll always be a boy."

Dawn put her hands on her hips. "God made me exactly as I am. And I'm not a boy!"

Again, the woman looked at Dawn's mother. She narrowed her eyes, and Dawn detected irritation bubbling inside her. The woman pursed her lips and shoved the rest of clothes into the bin. She turned back to Dawn, her face and neck blotched with red.

"I think we're done here," the woman said.

Dawn smiled. "Could I have a receipt, please?"

The woman pulled out a pad, scribbled something on it and handed a piece of paper to Dawn.

"Thank you," she said. She turned to leave with her mother but stopped, spun around, and addressed the Goodwill woman one last time.

"Do you have kids or grandkids?" she asked.

The corners of the woman's mouth had pulled into a frown. "That's none of your business."

"Because if you do, be sure to love them, no matter who or what they are. Bye."

She waved, then turned and wrapped an arm around her mother's waist as the two of them strolled out and into the sunshine that poured down on the Central Valley.

Noche Buena

The December fog had rolled in as it tended to do on winter nights in the San Joaquin Valley, its velvet thickness seductive yet deadly. One year, there was a forty-car pileup on Highway 99 and five people died, making not just state but national news. I stepped out into the backyard, pajama clad and hoodied, and sipped on my morning coffee. I couldn't see the houses across the pond from me—I could barely see the pond—and I thought of that first driver in the forty-car accident, who hit his brakes for some reason, and then the driver behind must have missed the taillights, and so on down the line of cars until the fog took its quota of human sacrifice. I thought that maybe people had learned their lesson—that the fog was indiscriminate and didn't care how fast or how slow people drove, what they looked like, who depended on them. But people don't always learn their lesson.

The patio door slid open behind me.

"Aren't you cold out here?" my husband asked.

I shook my head. "Not really."

He wrapped his arms around me and rocked me gently.

"Well, I think you should come inside. It's *La Noche Buena* and we have to decorate the tree." Christmas Eve. *La Noche Buena*,

'The Good Night.' I had taught my husband this and he liked to say it because it sounded pretty. He offered a gentle squeeze and then went back inside. I took one last look at the fog and wondered if it felt guilt or remorse for killing people, if it had any feelings at all.

...

The Christmas tree stood tall in the family room in all its naked greenness. I tended to over decorate, as my husband reminded me each year, and my penchant for eight-foot trees was legendary—recorded in annual photos and videos, and in the jokes from my friends, who referred to me as a size-queen for Douglas firs. As I studied her majesty, I envisioned the hundreds of tiny lights that would soon drape her body—mini-supernovas flinging starlight onto crystal and glass ornaments, a dazzling universe of festivity and spirit—and it occurred to me how transitory it all was, how these twelve days would end on January 6, how it would all begin again in three-hundred and sixty-five days with a new tree standing there, waiting for me with outstretched boughs, silently requesting her festive garb.

Growing up, I didn't know we were poor. I didn't discover that until the age of five, when a kindergarten friend invited me to his house for a sleepover on the other side of the highway. He lived in a real neighborhood, with manicured lawns, painted shutters, and driveways free of oil stains. Inside, his house smelled of scents that I would learn later in life were lavender and sage, the lingering ghosts of candles his mother burned regularly. Family portraits and giclée art dotted the robin's-egg walls. The furniture was new, carefully selected to make sense in an eclectic sort of way. When it was time to go to bed, we crawled into fresh sheets and his mother clicked the electric blanket to the low setting to keep us warm. I had never heard of an electric blanket before. The next day, I trudged back to my reality in the old farmhouse we rented because my dad had lost our real house to a gambling debt. I took in our mismatched furniture that had been donated by family members—because not only had we lost the house, but we'd also lost everything in it and the family car. I lay on the rollaway bed that barely fit into my closet-sized bedroom. I looked up at peeling wallpaper, pasted up decades before, revealing rotted wood in places. I closed my eyes and pictured my friend's house, wondering what it would be like to live like him, be him, have his parents. I spent many hours alone in my room conjuring a life different from my own, imagination becoming my most treasured childhood friend.

* * *

By lunchtime, we had finished the tree but, as was our custom, we waited until evening cocktails to place the star on top. My husband had come up with that ritual, saying it was the tradition in his family as long as he could remember. Because he was a good five inches taller than me, and I had a healthy fear of ladders, he always did the honor while I stood there with a glass of zinfandel, holding it up so that the tree lights burst through its deep red heart like garnets on fire. We didn't have such rituals growing up. Christmas tended to be a hollowed-out holiday as I wondered where we might wind up on December 25th, whether Uncle Jesse would invite us back after the year before when my dad stole one-hundred dollars from my uncle's cigar box and took off with a six pack of Budweiser. My father's drinking and gambling kept us perpetually in debt, and my mother's inability to move on kept us locked in a cycle of worrying about making rent.

As I made sandwiches, I stopped to look out the window above the sink. I had expected the fog to lift by then, but it hadn't, and I wondered if that was an omen. The roads would not be safe, so I texted my sister not to come for our yearly Christmas Eve dinner if the fog hadn't dissipated by mid-afternoon. I couldn't bear the thought of losing my sister to the fog, letting it claim her somewhere on the highway between my house and where she lived twenty miles away. We'd had enough loss in our family already.

The winter after I turned six, my mother finally got the idea that we would be better off living with our grandparents. They had little money, having emigrated from Mexico during the Revolution, and having worked the fields and dairies in California until they'd saved enough money to buy a small house in Sunnyvale. They were simple people, who still barely spoke English, but they were kind and believed that family was everything, readily taking me and my sister in while my mother sorted out her life. I was too young to know that sorting her life out meant taking up with another man. This fueled my dad's drinking even more. It was only much later that I realized my mother relished the conflict, probably thrived on it. Some people are like that. Conflict is their drug of choice, and they inject it into their lives. As part of this addiction, mother gave as good as she got, slapping and punching our dad after one of his binges, one time cracking his arm with a rolling pin she'd been using to make tortillas. As I matured, I wondered who was the dynamite and who was the fuse in that relationship, and I secretly prayed that I'd inherited none of their tendencies.

It was Christmas Eve when my father showed up at my grandparents' house. A gentle fog had crept in that night to settle on most of the South Bay. My dad pounded on the door and demanded to be let in. My grandmother went to answer, and I—half curious, half afraid—followed her, partially hiding behind her bulky frame as she muttered in Spanish that this didn't sound good. When she cracked the door, my father crashed his way through, slamming her against the wall and sending me tumbling after her. He brandished a gun and shouted for my mother, but of course, she was out with her man. My dad reached down and grabbed me, yanking my arm so that I winced.

"You're coming with me!" And he put the gun to my back to let my grandparents know he was not to be stopped.

My sister dashed out of the bedroom and screamed when she saw us. By this time, I was crying and pulling to get away, but my dad's grip was wrench tight. I caught a mix of booze and cigarettes, a smell I easily recognized, so I knew he'd been on a binge, probably losing his paycheck to guys in some backroom who saw him as an easy mark. He dragged me to his car and shoved me into the front seat, pointing the gun at me.

"You stay right there!"

He jumped in, threw the car in gear, and took off down the street. Through my tears, I saw houses and Christmas lights whizz by, blurs of color visible through the light fog, and inside my head screams of fear alternated with thoughts of wanting to be in any of those houses and not in that car. I don't think we made it past a mile when flashing red lights signaled that cop cars had pulled in front and behind, blocking us from moving in any direction. A bull-horned voiced boomed.

"Exit the vehicle with your hands in the air!"

My dad jumped from the car, gun raised. I heard shots and covered my ears and closed my eyes. Then I felt someone pulling me from the car.

"Come on, little fella," a male voice said softly. "It's okay."

* * *

I poured the zinfandel and made my way into the living room. My husband waited, ladder ready, star in hand.

"Here's to *La Noche Buena*," he said, lifting his glass. I smiled. He handed me his wine, then I watched him climb the ladder to place the star on top of the tree.

"Ta da," he said.

I stood there, studying the tree and holding both glasses. I brought mine up, peered through the wine to let the lights dazzle me through its jammy redness. But this time, I didn't see jewels set off by starlight. Instead, I was looking at peeling wallpaper, old Christmas lights on houses, and the flashing lights of cop cars. I took a sip and pushed myself to focus on the moment. My husband descended, removed the ladder, and then we both settled onto the sofa. I let my head rest against his shoulder.

"Another beautiful tree, hon," he said.

I simply nodded. Outside the fog remained thick.

Home

Snow fell softly on a late November evening in Michigan, quiet and without fuss, as though sneaking in to surprise everyone the next morning. The house was dark, save the spectral glow of the lamp beside my bed. I'd just given up trying to read and was ready to slip into pre-sleep thoughts about the day, the kinds of thoughts that spill over each other such that, as time passed, I wouldn't quite know if I'd actually thought about anything. And sleep—like the snow outside—would slowly and quietly cover me, and I'd be thankful for not having to be in control of anything.

The phone rang.

"Nick?"

I pulled myself from the half-sleep that had settled over me. "Hi, sis. I…I was just going to bed."

There was a pause—one of those pauses indicating something not good. The last time I got that kind of call was from my partner, who was away at a conference: *I have something to tell you.* That's how he eased into the end of our relationship. *I have something to tell you.*

"What's up?" I asked.

The years had not mellowed my sister's bluntness. "Mom died."

I pinched the bridge of my nose and tightly shuttered my eyes.

"Aunt Chris was there with her." My sister's voice was controlled, even. "She's the one who called me."

I wasn't sure what to feel. My mother had been sick for some time. On my last visit, the cancer had spread to her brain and choked away her sense of time and space.

"Johnny, I'm glad you're here," Mom said to me as I sat next to her bed, calling me by her youngest brother's name. Johnny had been dead for twenty years, another victim of cancer. Why had she conjured him instead of any of her other thirteen siblings?

"I'll check on flights first thing in the morning," I said to my sister. "Love you."

"Love you."

I hung up. I turned off the lamp and looked out the sliding door of my bedroom. As dark as it was, I could see the faint outline of snow falling. I thought how wonderful snowflakes were, how they were nature's perfect six-sided creations gently dropping from the clouds. And I thought how snow could make the bleakest landscape glisten with white beauty as a morning sun broke through clouds. Then I thought how we all could become snowflakes when we died. After our last breath, flesh and bone release molecules, and the light ones—the single and newly liberated H2Os—rise into the air. Some drift and move sideways, but others keep rising and rising until they mingle with the cold upper troposphere thousands of feet above the earth. They join others to form delicate, frozen crystallites, and then gently—ever so gently—spiral their way back down to cover roofs, to cling to pine needles, to land on people's tongues.

As I turned into my pillow and closed my eyes, I wondered how many people had landed on my tongue on any winter day.

* * *

I have often thought of life as rooms in a house. As the years advance, we move from chamber to chamber. We close a door, and the hinges creak to let us know we are leaving one space and entering a new one. Some rooms are warm with rich paneled walls, buttery leather sofas, and crackling fireplaces. Hundreds of books may line shelves, and lamps may cast golden glows in the corners and onto the ceiling. Other rooms are cold, with yellowed wallpaper and baseboards saddened by scuffmarks and chipped paint. A musty smell hangs in the air and enters your lungs as you pace in circles because there is nowhere to sit, no place to stop and rest.

As I sat on the plane, sipping chardonnay and catching glimpses of others in the first-class section, I thought of the rooms that made up my childhood and how I was happy to hear the hinges creak when I turned eighteen and left for college. I couldn't remember a time when my parents didn't argue, didn't fight, didn't use their fists and hands on each other. One time my father hurled a glass coffee pot. My mother dodged, but it smacked against a kitchen cabinet and sent a shower of glass shards in all directions, like exploding shrapnel. I screamed and my sister grabbed me, pulling me into the living room, spinning me around to see if I'd been hurt. I had no wounds—no external wounds—so she pulled me by my five-year-old hand into the bedroom and told me to stay, then closed the door behind herself as she ventured back into the war zone. Of course, I heard more fighting, more yelling, my sister pleading, until the back door slammed, and the car engine fired up—the crunch of gravel in the driveway telling me that someone was leaving. I crawled into bed and curled up. I prayed to the Virgin Mary as I'd been taught by my grandmother, saying Hail, Mary after Hail, Mary, finally drifting into the chaos of pre-sleep thoughts until dreams took me to rooms in other people's lives.

I landed in San Jose and picked up my rental car. I'd already called my sister and she gave me the mortuary information. It had been three decades since I'd left the South Bay and, on the drive, I felt out of place. This was the town where I'd grown up, the place that had claimed me for so long, but it had changed. The street names were the same, yes, but some had been widened, even to boulevard status, and the orchards that once dotted the valley were long gone. Instead, buildings, malls, and mile after mile of asphalt and concrete carpeted this once agricultural part of the Bay Area. As I took it all in, I felt alien, and I wondered what it was like for kids growing up here now, in this urbanized and push-and-pull city. It was home but it wasn't.

It reminded me of the time I'd run into my ex after not seeing him for almost fifteen years. I was attending a conference on bilingualism at which I was a featured speaker. I had given my talk earlier in the day and was seated at a hotel bar relaxing after a long day of attending talks and hobnobbing with other academics. Someone slid onto the stool next to me, and when I heard my name, I turned. At first, I wondered who he was, taking in the circles under his faded blue eyes, the pronounced crow's feet, and the protruding gut. As the realization settled in, I said, "Oh, hi, Tim." A singular question occupied me while we drank wine and pretended to be friends: This was the man I had loved and lived with for twelve years and who had left me for a twenty-two-year-old after I turned forty?

Navigating the streets of Santa Clara, I felt like I was sitting at that bar, turning to find a part of my past that was barely recognizable.

When I arrived at the funeral home, my sister was standing outside the entrance. I didn't know she'd taken up smoking again, thinking her addiction had been vanquished some ten years before. She threw her cigarette down and crushed the butt under the toe of her Nike running shoes, then ambled toward me with that walk that our mother would not-so-teasingly describe as a truck driver's gait.

"No delays?" she asked as she embraced me.

"Nope. The weather cooperated and here I am."

She looked me up and down, studying me to see if I'd changed from the last time we'd seen each other. "You need to come home more often."

"This is not home." I tried to sound neutral but I'm sure just a bit of irritation leaked through the words. She ignored it if it had. The truth was, I avoided trips to California, especially to visit my mother. A trip about every three years was the most I could handle.

"You ready?" she asked.

I nodded.

"Come." She hooked her arm into mine and led me inside.

In spite of my age, I'd only been to two funeral homes. When I was eight years old, my mother insisted that I accompany her to the funeral of a young girl who had been killed by her own father and his friend, both of whom had escaped from prison. During a ransacking of the girl's house, she and her mother arrived and the two men—high on a combination of drugs, booze, and malice—strangled the mother and ran a barbecue fork through the girl's throat. As I looked at her coffined body dressed in a white communion gown, I realized she was about my age. For weeks, I couldn't shake the image of that girl from my thoughts, and I began to wonder when I would die, and how it would happen. Would, I also get skewered on a barbecue fork? Eventually, the image crept away to live in some dark recess of my mind, and I stopped thinking about death, but I never set foot in a funeral home again—until my father died.

We spoke with the director who assured us that our mother

was being well cared for, and when I reminded him that she was dead and not sick, he backtracked and said, "We are properly preparing her for the ceremony."

I turned to my sister. "Ceremony?"

"Yes. It will be just us. And Aunt Chris."

"But I thought she wanted to be cremated."

"She did. But you can still have a ceremony."

I didn't think it would be much of ceremony with only three people present. My mother was estranged from her siblings, except Chris, her penchant for fighting not being confined to her relationship with our father—and he had died many years before. He'd hanged himself from a patio rafter during one of their brawls as she taunted him. "I dare you! I dare you!" Him sitting there, the noose dangling from above like a partially coiled boa waiting to slip around its prey. He scrambled up onto the picnic table, grabbed the noose and pushed his head through. He shouted, "Look what you make me do!" and leapt from the table. I had been watching from a seated position on the lawn, not believing anything would really happen, that this would end like all other fights with one of them storming off. I charged and grabbed his legs to hoist him, to defy gravity, defy the rope. I was only ten and not strong enough.

"Let him go," my mother said.

I screamed and swung at her. She slapped me. By the time my sister ran from the house to see what the fuss was, my dad was limp like a wilted leaf ready to drop from a tree limb. When the police came, we told the story my mother had sworn us to: that we found him dead.

Much later in life, I understood that the day my dad died, my childhood had been stolen. I grew distant from my family. I let books become my world, spending more time reading than with friends at school, and at the age of eighteen, I packed up and left for college. I had to put miles between myself and the past. And I continued to do so, until after graduate school, I wound up on the other side of the country.

But the past eventually finds you, no matter where you live.

• • •

We finished planning with the director, setting the ceremony for two days later, and my sister and I headed for a local bar. I eyed her over my martini, taking in her sixty years, five years my senior. Had we already lived that long? How many rooms had we passed through on our way to this day? Her hair had begun to pepper, and years of California sun, combined with her affinity for gardening, fishing, and camping, had parchmented her face so that she looked ten years older than she was.

"So, how's Dee?" I asked.

"Fine. She's home doing the usual."

That meant my sister-in-law was busy cleaning and organizing things in the house, her OCD not as pronounced as it once was but still present enough that not a speck of dust could be found in their house.

"We have the guest room ready for you."

I twirled the stem of my martini glass. "Jen, what are we going to do at the ceremony?"

"What do you mean?"

"Aren't funeral services for celebrating someone's life?"

She didn't answer right away and instead took a sip of her wine. After a beat, she said, "I know." She looked at me. "And I also know why you moved away. Why you've spent all these years somewhere else."

I wondered if she really did know. After all, she had stayed. For some reason, she'd remained anchored to this town, to the rooms we grew up in. I glanced toward the large window overlooking the sun-spilt parking lot, the array of cars shooting slivers of light off polished chrome, people wearing sunglasses in late November. I thought of where I'd been the day before and how I wished it would snow in Santa Clara, cover everything in that brilliant fresh whiteness, make it all look different than it was. I would fall into it, make snow angels with my arms and legs.

    I'd let the dead touch my tongue.

Beneath

Marion yanked the still-burning cigarette from her lips and tossed it to the ground, stomping on it with cockroach-killing ferocity. Over three decades of smoking, five attempts to quit, and a nagging cough aggravated by almond tree pollen had taken their toll. At fifty-two, she looked like someone smack in the center of middle age, and there was no way she could pass herself off as someone younger. Yet, she didn't consider herself unattractive. After all, her hair hadn't turned gray yet, and her blue eyes often sparkled with mischief. And she hadn't gained more than two pounds since her twenty-first birthday, probably thanks to her mother's genes. That side of the family tended to be slim. But she did lament that her forties were behind her, and that the bathroom mirror reminded her every day that sixty was a short trip down the road.

She popped a tic-tac in her mouth to scour away the taste of smoke and hurried toward the front door of The Fairway, a restaurant-bar on the golf course in the town of Mañana. She had the lunch shift today and needed to be on the floor by eleven. Sonny had come in at ten to do the prep work for the day, which meant she would leave at two. Marion would then work alone to prep for the dinner rush. She pushed through the glass doors and pasted on a smile for the bartender and Kevin, the owner, as they greeted her.

"Happy Wednesday," she said as she pulled her apron from a hook and tied it around her waist. Sonny was busy at the server station, rolling silverware into napkins. "Need any last-minute help?"

"I'm almost done," Sonny said, "but sure."

The place was relatively quiet—at least for a restaurant. The overhead music had not been turned on yet, and the only sound came from the kitchen. Marion heard the cooks stirring, banging pots, heard their voices as they cajoled each other. ¡Ándale, pendejo! ¡Así no! and Pues, cabrón. Hazlo tú, entonces. Over the years, she'd picked up a few Spanish words here and there, but most of the time it was background noise for her—just like the din of overlapping conversations and the sound of silverware scraping plates that filled the restaurant during lunch and dinner.

She sidled up beside Sonny, placed knives and forks on napkins, then rolled them like she was a line cook making taquitos or a sushi chef making hand rolls. The place was devoid of customers, the first didn't normally trickle in until eleven-thirty—what they all called the early-birds, those eaters who like to beat the twelve o'clock rush and probably didn't have jobs with defined break times or lunch hours. Mañana was full of them, especially over at The Palms—the gated community that backed up onto the golf course. A lot of retired folks and work-at-home types lived there.

Marion sometimes pondered what it would be like to live in The Palms, with its $400,000+ homes, ponds, parks, and private streets. She lived on the other side of Mañana, in a 1950s one-story ranch with two bedrooms and one bath, where carports and one-car detached garages were the norm. She was a working gal, surviving on minimum wage and tips, and $100,000 in insurance money she'd inherited from her parents who'd died in an automobile accident two years prior. She'd kept telling her dad he was too old to drive, but he was set in his ways, and they took off one morning in the fog for her mother's eye appointment in Fresno. Their accident had made the local news.

She and Sonny finished the silverware just as the bartender Cindy turned on the overhead music and the first customer came in. He was a regular and his name was Jack Daniel, which everyone teased him about because he hated whiskey and had never set foot in Tennessee in his life. Mid-fifties and living alone, he was a good customer and a great tipper, and Marion wondered why some woman hadn't snatched him up. Or maybe some woman had, but the relationship hadn't work out. Her own marriage hadn't. She called out to him.

"Hey, Jack. Pick a seat and I'll be with you in a minute."

Sonny winked at her with that "uh-huh" expression, signaling she knew that Marion would flirt with Jack. *And why not?* Marion thought. *We're both single and old enough to know the difference between fun and trouble.* She winked back, poured an ice water for Jack, and then headed to his table.

"So, how're you doing today, handsome."

He smiled. "You always make me happy when you call me that."

"I calls 'em as I sees 'em."

He chuckled.

"Gonna start with your usual?"

"You know me so well," he replied.

The usual was a bloody Mary with extra spice. She headed for the computer where she placed the order for Cindy and then waltzed through the restaurant and into the breezeway that led to the bar, knowing that without any other customers, Cindy would prepare the drink in no time. Sure enough, within two minutes, Marion placed the drink on Jack's table. He immediately took a long sip.

"Ahhh," he said, then dabbed at his mouth. "Wish you could sit with me and enjoy one."

"Maybe one of these days," she said with a smile, "when I'm not working."

He pursed his lips. "I said this to you before, Marion, but I just don't understand how your husband could up and leave you."

She brushed an errant hair from her forehead then placed her hand on her hip. "Well, some men, when they get to a certain age, like a car with fewer miles on it."

"Damn fool, if you ask me." He took another sip, then picked up the menu and perused the lunch plates.

Ray—or, as she often referred to her husband, that no good son of a bitch—had disappeared just a year before, and *good riddance* were the only words that rolled off her tongue at the time.

"So, what you got a hankering for?" she asked Jack.

"I'm thinking the turkey melt," he said, stroking his neatly trimmed beard with an absent-minded gesture.

"Perfect."

Marion spun on her heels and scurried off to the computer and punched in the order. She knew Jack well enough to know that by the time the sandwich was ready, he'd have downed his bloody Mary and would be ready for a second one. She glanced over and sure enough, he'd already made it through half his drink. She punched in an order for another but added a note for Cindy to hold off until she gave her the signal. From behind her, Sonny whispered into her ear.

"He really likes you."

"You think?" she replied.

She turned to see her fellow server grinning. "You should go out with him. It's been a year, you know."

"I'll consider it."

Before they could continue, a party of four appeared. Sonny greeted the group with menus in hand and told them to sit wherever they wanted. Marion appreciated her. They worked well together, didn't fight over customers, and had long ago established that when just the two of them worked a shift, they would split tips, fifty-fifty. Mañana was far from being a high-rollers town, but the regulars who came in when the two of them worked lunch or dinner together did not shy away from giving a twenty-percent tip.

Marion glanced at the kitchen, and the cook gave her the one-minute signal with his index finger. She hustled to the bar, but Cindy had seen her coming, and by the time she arrived, Jack's second bloody Mary was poured and ready to serve. Marion thanked her and headed back to the kitchen window. The cook had just placed the turkey melt on the counter. She retrieved it and then bustled over to Jack.

"Here you go, darling," she said. She placed the sandwich with its heaping side of sweet potato fries in front of him. Then she switched out his empty glass for the fresh beverage she'd carried in her other hand.

"Ahh, you spoil me," he replied as he eyed the frosty drink. He looked up at her. "I'm still hoping for a date, you know."

She tilted her head. "I just may take you up on that."

She winked and then hurried over to a group of three women that had just appeared at the entrance to the dining area. Regulars like Jack, she called them The Ladies Who Lunch. They came in once a week from The Palms and always ordered glasses of chardonnay. They'd once told her they'd met each other while serving on the Friends of the Library. Marion liked that. While not college educated, she was an avid reader, liking thrillers as well as murder mysteries and stories that had twists and unreliable narrators. If she could only write herself, she sometimes mused. She believed her single talent was the ability to strum the guitar and eke out a ditty with the hint of a rasp in her voice. She'd done karaoke at the Lantern, a local dive bar off Highway 99 just a few miles from her house, and people told her she was good. She always shrugged off such compliments, knowing that if her husband had found out about her occasional nights at the bar, he would've put a stop to them damn quick.

After she handed menus to the ladies, she asked if they wanted their usual wine.

"Can't think of a better way to lunch," one of them said.

"You know what I like to say," another chimed. "Wine a little!"

They giggled in a way that embodied their camaraderie, and Marion left them to go about her routine, a grin spreading across her own face. And so the hour went, as the restaurant filled, lunch plates came out the kitchen window, and drinks seemed to fly from the bar. She stopped by to check on Jack.

"I guess you were hungry," she said looking down at his empty plate. She picked it up. "Anything else?"

"Just the check and your phone number."

She smiled at this well-worn line of his, and as usual, she ignored it. She turned and dropped the dirty dish and silverware into the bussing tub before heading to the computer to print out his bill. She delivered it to him, patted him on the shoulder saying she'd see him again soon, and then hurried over to a table to respond to a customer who had just gestured to get her attention.

· · ·

At home that night, she kicked off her shoes and, in stockinged feet, padded her way to the fridge and retrieved an ice-cold Michelob Ultra. She pushed through the screened-in backdoor and dropped onto a plastic Adirondack-style chair on the porch. She propped her feet on a small table and looked out onto the garden behind her house. The air was comfortable in low seventies on this early June evening. Soon, daytime temperatures would climb into the nineties and with July, the onslaught of endless days of triple digits. She set her beer down, fished for a cigarette and flicked her lighter. Then she reached into a pocket and pulled out a piece of paper. Jack had slipped her a note earlier—not the first time he'd done so. She usually crumpled them up and tossed them, but she'd kept this one. It amused her as she reread it.

> *I don't want the latest model off the line. I like your car.*
>
> *Won't you give me a chance?*

He'd added his phone number as he'd done in the past. She smiled, put the note back in her pocket, and then picked up her beer and swigged down a good mouthful.

"Well, Mr. Jack Daniel. I just may give you a chance."

She looked out at the rose bushes lined up next to the one-car garage. They'd bloomed this year like they never had before. She thought it must've been the special fertilizer she'd put down the year before. Truth was, her husband hadn't left her for a twenty-something. That was just a story she told, and people ate it up. More than one woman commiserated because they'd been dumped by their husbands, too.

"Something about a man when he hits fifty," a former server at The Fairway told her the previous fall, just before Halloween. "It's like they get this itch because they're afraid of growing old and dying. They think some young woman is going to keep them alive forever."

That's not what happened with Ray. She never let on to anyone that he drank too much and was prone to fits of shouting and hitting her. It hadn't started out that way. Their first ten years were good—sometimes very good—as they made their way through their thirties while settling into a life together. She loved him and believed he loved her, even if it wasn't with the intensity of Romeo and Juliet. But it was love, nonetheless—tender kisses, occasional passionate lovemaking, and yearly romantic getaways. Her favorite times were when they sat on the back porch, looking out at the yard on a summer night, making plans for the future while crickets chirped, filling the air with their nighttime mating music.

Then, when he rounded forty, Ray changed. At first, it was just arguments and fights that he picked about this or that, stupid things, really, like who should do what around the house or who forgot to put gas in the car. He began drinking more than usual, and it wasn't until a good five years had gone by that she realized he was a bona fide drunk with a half-bottle of scotch gone by the end of every night. She asked him more than once what was going on, what had happened. He'd peer at her through a bleary-eyed stupor.

"I don't know what the fuck you're talking about," he'd say, and then go back to watching TV.

She knew some men went through mid-life crises, but didn't they have affairs? Buy new cars? Her efforts at getting him to open up were futile, and she settled into a loveless existence, spending more time alone in the bedroom reading her mysteries and thrillers than with her husband in the living room watching senseless game shows and sports programs.

When he hit fifty, the physical abuse started. At first, it was slaps on the face.

"Why isn't my shirt ironed?" he'd bellow, holding the garment close to her. Then, smack! "I expect a wife to do her chores!"

Slaps progressed to punches—on the arm, the belly, sometimes on her lower back, sending her kidneys into spasmic pain.

"See what you make me do!" he said once while punishing her for not filling up the car with gas. "I have to keep you in line!"

Marion confided in her mother, who told her that all couples go through trials and tribulations, and that she shouldn't give up too easily.

"You married him for better or for worse," her mother said. "Maybe you need to think about what you're doing to contribute to the situation."

Marion took that to heart, looked at ways to be more attentive, to anticipate Ray's needs. For two years, she endured the wallops, the bruises on her arms and back—all the while hoping he would change, that her life could end up like a Hallmark movie and they'd live the way they had in their thirties. But as for those vows her mother had spoken of, there was no better; just worse. Thoughts of leaving him nagged at her, mental gnats flitting around her mind—along with imagined scenes of how her life could be different. The one saving grace from that marriage gone to hell was that they never had children.

One evening she came home from work, and there he was as usual, parked in front of the television with a scotch to one side and a jumbo bag of Lays potato chips in his lap. His gut hung over his pants and crumbs had gathered on his t-shirted chest. She slung her purse onto the kitchen table, eyed the dirty dishes in the sink, and sighed. He looked up at her.

"Don't start with that sighing shit," he said. "I work for a living, and I can do what I want at home."

"I work for a living, too." And as soon as the words had tumbled from her lips, she knew what was coming.

He stood, tossing the bag of chips onto the sofa, and lumbered toward her.

"You got a smart mouth on you, don't you?" Spittle flew from his lips. "You're just looking for me to teach you another lesson."

She backed up as he loomed nearer, his fists clenched. When her butt brushed up against the counter, he charged. Something inside her cracked. A welled-up dam of emotions burst, and a mix of rage and frustration surged and took control of her actions, pushing against her like a thirty-foot wall of water swallowing up everything in its sight. She grabbed the closest weapon she could see—a carving knife that lay on the drainboard next to the sink. His eyes went wide when she plunged it into his belly. She shoved as hard as she could. Then she twisted the blade. Warm blood squirted onto her hand. He cried out.

"What the fuck…?"

She leaned into him, her hand firmly clenched on the handle of the knife, driving it in even deeper.

"No more," she whispered into his ear. "No fucking more."

He stumbled backward, mouth agape, staring down at his bloodied abdomen. He fell against a kitchen chair, groping for a perch that he couldn't find, and then crumbled as his knees buckled. He hit the linoleum floor with a thud, hids eyes still wide. He gasped one time before his head lolled to one side, a vacant gaze focused on nothing.

Marion put her hand to her mouth. A slight moan escaped her as she stared at her dead husband. Her mind raced as confusing thoughts tumbled against each other. Her body shook. She drew in a few deep breaths to steady herself.

"Stop. Think this through," she finally said.

Still trembling, she dragged over a kitchen chair, the legs scraping against the linoleum floor like claws rasping against a slippery slope. She slowly lowered herself onto the seat and sat there looking at Ray. Minutes ticked off on the clock hanging on the wall behind him, the second hand sweeping in a jerky motion around its face. She became aware that the television was still on. She stood, walked into the living room, and shut it off.

When she returned to the kitchen, an idea formed in her head. It came from one of the thrillers she'd read.

"Okay," she said. "You can do this. You will do this."

Thoughts raced through her mind. He was an only child. His parents were dead. He'd moved here from Missouri and had no relatives close by. He often missed work due to his drinking. She could make up any story she wanted.

"Yes, you can do this," she repeated.

She went out to the garage and fetched a saw, a tarp, and several large trash bags. Then she hurried back to the kitchen, placed all the items on the table before opening a drawer and pulling out a meat cleaver. She looked at Ray one last time.

"You deserved this, you know."

Then she set about her task.

* * *

Marion took another pull on her beer, sucked in one last drag off her cigarette, and then crushed it out in the ashtray on the small table next to her. She stood, stretched her neck to work out the kinks from pulling an eight-hour shift, and then descended into the backyard and strode over to the roses.

"You're doing pretty good this year, girls," she said.

She reached for a few flowers and stroked their soft white petals, then brought her hand to her nose. She closed her eyes and inhaled the sweetness of the aroma lingering on her fingertips. Then she looked down at the ground and imagined the bits and pieces of her husband that lay beneath.

She smiled, then returned to her chair on the porch. She picked up the phone and punched in a number.

"Hi, Jack. Guess who…"

Elena

MAY 31

The psychologist says that writing is good therapy, that it will help me see things more clearly. I doubt it. Besides, I'm not crazy and I'm not sick. But I'll do what he says. It will make him happy.

I live in Mañana, California, but the clinic is in Merced. I come from a long line of Catholic families. I think that's important to mention given that I'm here because of the Virgin Mary. You'd think that having a religious tradition would help in this case, help my parents understand. But it hasn't.

I'm seventeen years old. My parents had me hospitalized. I guess I'm resentful, but not just for being here. I'm resentful because my parents don't believe me. They think they're doing the right thing.

But I keep saying, I'm not crazy and I'm not sick.

I don't suffer from hallucinations like the doctor says. I'm not that imaginative—or creative. And I'm certainly not a liar. I mean, sure, I tell little white lies. But everyone does that—kids and adults. Those are necessary when you don't want to hurt someone's feelings or when you need to keep someone from knowing something until they're ready. But there is no lie in what I've been telling my parents, the doctor, the priest. Everything is true.

I'm here because of the Virgin. She comes to me at night and speaks to me.

* * *

JUNE 2

I think my parents are desperate—desperate for me to "get better." I'm sure they pray for me. They probably have the priest asking for special prayers at mass just for me. I know they pray for my brothers, but for different reasons.

Eduardo—Eddie—is a student at UC Davis. He's working on a graduate degree in sociology. Of the three of us kids, he's probably the smartest. I do well in school and want to go to college, but I'm not as intellectual as Eddie is. He lives with his boyfriend, Jimmy. My parents are very traditional, especially my dad. They've never invited Jimmy to the house, and Eddie won't come for the holidays or visit in his free time unless he can bring his boyfriend. So, he and I talk on the phone, and sometimes he talks to my mother. My father refuses to speak to him.

Eddie has always believed in me. He says, "Elena, you can be anything and do anything you want in life. No one can tell you otherwise." He's already come down from Davis to visit me in the clinic. Jimmy came with him. I like him a lot. He smiles all the time, which make his blue eyes sparkle. People say that eyes are the window to the soul. If so, I see a good soul in Jimmy, a joyful soul. I get why Eddie loves him.

My oldest brother Ernesto died in the Middle East ten years ago. His truck hit a land mine in Afghanistan. Everyone was devastated, my dad especially. I don't think he's ever really recovered from the loss. Ernesto was the first born. Sometimes I think my father takes his grief out on Eddie.

As for me, I'd like to be a veterinarian. Animals are honest and simple. I think it's easy to communicate with them if you want to. Sometimes it's easier to communicate with animals than with humans. My favorite saint is Saint Francis. He's the protector of animals. At home, I have a retablo of him over my headboard. I like to think he watches over me the way he watches over animals.

But it's not Saint Francis who comes to visit me. It's the Virgin. I like to think that maybe he sent her. The two of them are up in heaven and he asks, "How's Elena doing" and maybe she says, "Okay, given the circumstances…" Perhaps I have a bit more imagination than I like to admit. Yet, her visits aren't imaginary. They're very real.

"Elena," she says to me in sweet tones, "I have an important message." And then she talks as she shows me things, things I don't understand.

I feel a need to record the images. Make them permanent so that I can show others. She tells me the world must believe. So I mark myself…

* * *

JUNE 3

I had a session with the psychologist this morning. He's a man in his forties, I think, decent looking with soft brown eyes. On his desk was a photo of him, a woman, and a boy about ten-years old. All of them sported big smiles, like they didn't have a care in the world. That made me wonder about him. He spends all day taking care of people with problems. Some of them are probably real nutjobs. Then, when the afternoon ends, he has to leave them behind and go home to a family and be a dad and a husband. Is there a switch in his mind? Once he leaves the clinic, does he just turn off what happened during the day, everything he's heard or seen?

"How are you today?" he asked me.

"Fine."

"May I see your arms?"

He smiled slightly after his examination.

"Nothing new. That's a good sign."

He and my parents claim I'm cutting myself, but they're wrong. I mark myself. There's a big difference.

"How are your dreams?" he asked.

Psychologists are fascinated by dreams. I think I disappoint my doctor. Sometimes I tell him I don't remember. That's what I said this morning.

"Elena, if we're going to progress in your therapy, you have to be honest with me."

"I don't need therapy." I know not to show too much emotion when we meet, so I kept my tone neutral.

"That's what you say. But your actions suggest the opposite." He jutted his chin at my arm.

I wanted to roll my eyes but refrained. I looked him squarely in the eye. "Look at you. Don't you mark yourself?"

I used the same gesture on him. I jutted my chin to indicate the tattoo on his left arm. It was a dragon, with claws extended—almost like it was in attack position. I thought it was an odd tattoo for someone whose job it was to help others.

"That's different," he said.

"How is it different? You mark yourself the same way I do. You just do it with ink."

He shifted in his seat. "Elena, we've had this conversation. Cutting yourself—"

I stopped him. "No! Not cutting. *Marking.*" That was the one time I let a bit of emotion show.

We looked at each other. I could tell he was studying me, but I was simply waiting for a response.

"Okay, then. Why do you *mark* yourself?"

"I've already told you. I've told my parents. I've told Father González."

"Yes. You say the Virgin tells you to."

I nodded.

"Then," he said, "can you explain to me what those markings mean?"

I traced them on my left arm with my right index finger. "I don't know. But somehow, they're important."

"Important?"

"The Virgin shows me things. These markings represent some kind of message."

"And what is the message?"

"I don't know," I replied. I traced the markings on my arm again, then looked up at him. "I'm sure the Virgin will soon reveal that to me. Then, I'll let you know." I glanced at the clock on his desk, then stood. "Our time is almost up. Thank you, Doctor."

I turned and left.

* * *

JUNE 4

Last night, the Virgin came to me in my room. It was midnight. She always comes at midnight. She once said that is the sacred hour, the time when night gives birth to morning.

She spoke to me. As usual, her tone was sweet and low, like a coo, the soft sound of a dove. I didn't see her, of course. I never see her. I only hear her.

Elena, my dear. I have something to show you.

And then she began to murmur. With my eyes closed, I listened. She spoke in Spanish, but then switched to another language. She always starts in Spanish and then changes. I have no idea what the other language is. I think it must be holy—the language of angels, of heaven, of God. Even though I don't know what she says, her words bathe me in peace and happiness. It's a happiness I never feel with my family and never feel with my friends or relatives. More than happiness, it's a kind of bliss. Maybe even ecstasy. Most people wouldn't think someone my age knows what ecstasy is, but I believe I do. It's complete and utter happiness, without limit. My heart slows when she speaks. My body feels light. It's as though the Virgin settles on my soul and her words mix with my blood and course through my veins.

My mind fills with images I don't recognize. Faces. Figures. Symbols. Yes, symbols. I don't know what they are or what they represent. But they are symbols.

Time passes slowly. I float above the Earth. I'm part of something much bigger than life itself. The images coalesce with the chaos that is the universe. I stop thinking and I disconnect from the world. And then…and then…I merge with the blackness we call "night." I cease to be myself.

This time, I woke up at seven in the morning. I rushed to the bathroom. I'd hidden a knife in the toilet tank. I sat on the floor and closed my eyes. And with the knife, I traced new lines in my skin.

They found me later, lying on the floor. I'd fainted. They must've thought it was a suicide attempt and rushed me to the emergency room. But none of them noticed the smile on my face or the contentment that enveloped me. Or maybe I was only smiling on the inside. It doesn't matter.

I was happy.

* * *

JUNE 5

My parents came to visit this morning.

"Elena!" my mother exclaimed. "What a fright you gave us!"

She spoke in Spanish, the language we tended to use at home. She leaned in and kissed me on the forehead and then sat in the chair near the bed. My father remained standing. He looked at the bandages on my arm, and I could see the sadness in his eyes—like he wanted to cry, but something kept the tears at bay. Do all men have a hard time with emotions? My brother Jimmy doesn't, but then, he and my dad couldn't be more different.

"I'm fine, Papá," I said. "Don't worry."

"Why…why…?" But he couldn't finish the question that hung on his tongue: *Why are you doing this?*

"It's not what you think," I said.

I looked at my mother. She focused on my expression, probably searching for the answer to my father's unspoken question.

"Mamá, really, I'm fine. I promise. I don't want to kill myself. I don't want to die. I'm not cutting myself. I've told you over and over. I'm marking myself, the way the Virgin shows me."

"Father González says you're confused," she said. "That maybe…"

She couldn't speak the words. But I could.

"That maybe I suffer from hallucination or worse. The Devil is tempting me."

Tears gathered in her eyes. Slowly, they descended. I reached for her hand.

"I understand why you don't believe me." I kept my voice calm. The last thing I needed to do was sound excited, or frustrated. That would only have reinforced their belief that I was sick. I continued.

"It's not easy to believe that the Virgin would talk to a seventeen-year-old girl from Mañana."

My mother pulled a tissue from her purse and dabbed at her eyes. My father remained immobile, like a statue, but with human eyes that were fixed on me.

"But don't you think the same thing happened to Joan of Arc?" I said. "Or with the kids at Lourdes or Fátima?" I could feel excitement in my voice, so I measured myself to stay calm and not appear agitated.

"And you, Mamá. And you, Papá. You both believe in the story of the Virgin of Guadalupe. Why would she appear to a poor Indian from the countryside but not to someone like me? Am I less than all these other people? It's sad, you know?"

"What?" my mother asked.

I locked my gaze on her. "That you prefer to believe the Devil is at work here and not the Virgin Mary."

"Elena, don't say such things." My mother pled, her eyes still glistening. "We don't believe that—"

"*I* believe you."

It was my brother, Eddie, in the doorway.

"Hi, Mamá. Hi, Papá."

He strode over to my mother and kissed her on the cheek. She offered him a light smile. My father looked at the floor. Eddie ignored the slight and approached my bed.

"Hi, sweetie," he said. He leaned in and hugged me.

I looked toward the door. "Jimmy didn't come with you?"

"He couldn't. He's turning in a late paper."

Jimmy studies philosophy and comparative religion. He's

fascinated by ancient civilizations. Like my brother, he's very smart and very dedicated.

My mother cleared her throat. "It's good to see you," she said to Eddie.

I saw something in her eyes, like she missed my brother. Or maybe it was sorrow I detected. I turned my attention to my dad. His gaze remained set on the floor, and I thought, *Adults! They can be such children sometimes!* My brother glanced at my arm.

"How are you doing?"

"I'm good. I'm trying to explain to Mom and Dad that it's not what they think."

Eddie nodded slowly. "Sometimes it's hard to get them to understand."

"Enough!" my father bellowed.

I looked at him. His narrowed eyes were focused on Eddie and his face had turned red.

"You can't come in here stirring things up!"

"Papá," I said, "Eddie was simply—"

My father raised his hand to cut me off. "I said enough. I'm going to the cafeteria." He turned to my mother. "When you are finished, you can find me there." He spun around and marched out of the room.

"Wow," Eddie said. A few seconds passed, and then he added, "Mamá, I'm sorry. I don't mean to cause any problems."

My mother stood. "Eduardo, you know that your father has difficulty in…in…"

"In accepting me?" Eddie said.

My mother cast her gaze down. After a few seconds, she looked up at me. "I should go tend to your father. I'll leave you and your brother to visit."

She gently patted my hand, and then Eddie and I were left alone.

"Elena, I'm sorry that—"

"Don't worry," I said, interrupting him. "Come. Sit next to me."

He took the seat my mother had just vacated.

"Do you want to see what brought me to the emergency room?"

He nodded.

"Okay," I said. "Last night the Virgin visited me again. At midnight, you know, as usual. And she said, 'My dear, I'm here…'"

I explained how she starts in Spanish and then switches to an unknown language. I described the collage of images, mostly symbols. As I continued the story, Eddie watched me with rapt attention, just the hint of a smile on his lips.

* * *

Eddie stayed with me for a while. I took off the bandages on my arm to show him.

"This is what I did before I came here." I pointed to the marking.

フ

"And this is the one I did last night."

ᛗ

Eddie peered down, taking in what he saw. After a few moments he asked if he could touch them.

"If you want," I said.

With his finger, he traced the first marking. Then the second. He looked like a scientist studying a new specimen.

"I can see why you say you mark yourself," he said. "When people cut themselves, they do so in straight lines." He demonstrated with one index finger slicing along his arm. "But these… these markings…they look like…"

He studied them some more. Then he took out his phone. "May I?"

"Sure, I guess. But what for?"

"I'm not sure." But the tone in his voice suggested he had some idea.

"You think they represent something, don't you?"

"Elena, I don't know," he said. "Something is going on that I don't quite understand. But you know I will always support you."

I smiled. "Thanks."

He snapped several photos. Then he told me he had to leave and that he would call me later. He kissed me on the cheek and then left.

* * *

During the night, the nurses watched me like sentinels. But the Virgin didn't come. I waited and waited, but nothing happened. I wondered why. Was it because of the nurses? Why would she care? She was the Virgin and could come any time she wanted. In any event, she only came as a voice. No one would see her.

I tried to sleep but couldn't. I thought about my parents' visit, the way that my dad had treated Eddie. He must see my brother as a failure, as some kind of insult to the family or the family name. All I see when I look at my brother is love. And now there's me. Did my parents see me as a failure, too? Something they are ashamed of? They've stuck me in this place, hoping I'll emerge different somehow, that I'll change.

But there's nothing to change.

A soft light filtered through the window of my room, and I studied the markings on my arm. Eventually, I drifted off to sleep, wondering what the Virgin wanted of me.

* * *

JUNE 8

Why are clinics so bland, so lifeless? I'm surrounded by white walls, linoleum floors without rugs, and drapes the color of wilted cornflowers. It's like the designer had no heart and decorated the place without passion. I might as well be in the desert—some sterile place where joy does not flourish, and the only feelings allowed are those the doctors want to till from the soil of damaged hearts and minds. I'd like to fill my room with color, make it look like springtime. Pinks, and purples, and bright greens. I'd redecorate the entire clinic. It should vibrate with happiness.

I've been here for a week now. I'm not the only young person, though. Rebecca is almost my age. She's sixteen and her parents deposited her here because she attempted suicide. I use the word "deposited" on purpose. Since she arrived, her parents have not come to see her. My guess is they view her attempt as an embarrassment—some kind of stain on the good name of their family.

She's a thin girl, with dark hair and brown eyes that have lost any sense of childish delight. I spoke with her, and she confessed she tried to hang herself. That's not a typical way for young girls to try to kill themselves. Much more typical is for them to take pills or to throw themselves from some high place. To be honest,

I don't understand suicide, and I told Rebecca that. We were sitting in the game room, alone.

"Sometimes, you don't feel like there's anything else," she said. Her voice rang hollow, like her lips mouthed the words but her thoughts were somewhere else.

"No," I answered. "We're not here to give up. We're here to fight, to face all the obstacles. Life is what we make of it."

These were words I'd learned from Eddie, but I believed them, and I meant them when I talked to Rebecca. She just looked at me, and then broke into tears. I hugged her and tried to calm her.

"No, no," I whispered. "Don't cry. You have friends here." I pulled back and held her face in my hands. "You have me. I'm your friend."

The voice of Father González interrupted us.

"It's good to have friends."

He stood in the doorway, dressed in his priestly attire, and it dawned on me: priests and nuns don't want to exhibit joy or happiness in the way they look. They wear black or some other lifeless color. How does that inspire anyone? Adding to the father's appearance were his perpetually tired eyes, surrounded by wrinkles and a fleshy face, all topped with pomaded gray hair.

"May I?" he asked.

No, I thought. *This is a private conversation.* But I said yes, of course, and he shuffled in. He looked at Rebecca.

"And you, young lady. What's your name?"

"Rebecca," she said. Her voice was barely audible. "Rebecca Ortiz."

The father approached us. "Well, it's a pleasure, Miss Ortiz."

He extended his hand. Slowly, Rebecca reciprocated, her movement tentative.

"Do you mind if I have a few moments alone with Miss Ramírez?"

It was a question, but coming from Father González, it was more of a demand. She stood. I reached for her hand and stopped her.

"Don't forget what we talked about," I said. "Okay?"

She nodded, and I let go. Then, with the lightest of steps, she left. Father Gonzalez's gaze followed her.

"She looks like a nice girl," he said.

"She is."

The truth was I didn't want to speak with the priest and hoped my flat tone conveyed my lack of interest. But it didn't. He turned to me and with a gesture asked permission to sit. I nodded.

"Elena, I'm here because I'm worried."

"About what?"

"About you." He studied me, the way the psychologist did. "What happened the other night?"

"Nothing."

He looked at my arm, then back at me. "Nothing?"

I narrowed my eyes a bit as I looked at him. "It's not what you think. I'm not here because I tried to kill myself."

"Then why are you here?"

I wanted to stand and leave. I was tired of explaining to everyone what had happened, what *was* happening. They didn't want to believe me. They could only believe what they wanted to, maybe were taught to. But I stayed.

"You know why," I said.

"Elena—"

"Father, you doubt that the Virgin would speak to someone like me. It makes no difference in how I tell the story. You will never believe me. So, why waste our time? Surely there must be someone else in need of your attention."

And without saying anything else, I stood and marched out. Leaving him by himself in that room without color, without life.

* * *

In the night, the Virgin came.
My dear. I'm here. Listen to me.
Then she spoke in that strange language. Images tumbled in my head. Symbols that repeated in threes. Two I recognized from before. One was new. After she left, I searched for something to mark myself. But the attendants are good at checking my room now. So, I took a crayon and drew what she showed me on a piece of paper. Tomorrow, I will find something in the cafeteria, and then transfer what she showed me to my arm.

* * *

JUNE 9

The psychologist came by my room late in the morning. His face was drawn.

"What's the matter, doctor?"

"You are very astute, Elena."

"I'm not astute," I responded. "I can see something in your expression. Anyone could see it."

He sat in the chair near my bed and lowered his gaze. "Something happened last night."

He paused, then looked at me. I don't know how but, in that moment, I knew why he was there.

"Something's happened to Rebecca," I said.

He remained silent, looking at me.

"She killed herself," I added.

Finally, he spoke. "I'm very sorry. I understand you were friends."

I swallowed. "I wanted to be her friend." I turned my attention to the window. The drapes were open, and I could see a cloudless blue sky outside. It beckoned, the sunlight pouring down on the world. So different from my sterile surroundings. I stared, not wanting to look at the doctor. "How did she do it?"

He hesitated. "Elena…"

I turned to face him. "Please. I would like to know."

He sighed and then brushed at his nose with his hand. "She, uh, she hanged herself with shoelaces. She'd been collecting them, it seems. We had no idea."

I closed my eyes. I tried to picture her as she was when we were together. I could see her eyes, and I remembered when I got her to laugh. I'd told a story about the time we let the frogs escape from biology class, how the kids were screaming for them to run for their lives and how the teacher shouted for us to stop. The image of her smile faded. I opened my eyes.

"Thank you, doctor.

He stood to leave.

"Wait," I said. "I want you to know something."

He turned toward me.

"I want you to understand that I have never wanted to hurt myself. And I have no intention of doing so now. I'll tell you what I told Rebecca. We're not on this Earth to give up, but to fight."

He nodded. "You are strong, Elena. I'm beginning to see that."

"One more thing, doctor."

"Yes?"

"Thank you again. I appreciate that you came in person."

He pursed his lips. "If at any time you want to talk about this…"

I didn't want to talk. I understood what Rebecca had done. I'd tried to persuade her, convince her about life, how important it was. But in the end, she did what she did. I would not blame myself. She was to blame—and perhaps all the people who'd failed her up until she'd arrived here.

No. I didn't need to talk to anyone.

During lunchtime, I stole a plastic fork. The staff thinks plastic utensils are harmless. They probably are, but I went to my room with my stolen treasure and in the afternoon, I pulled out the piece of paper with the symbol on it from last night. I carved the symbol onto my skin using one of the tines from the fork.

And while I did that, I thought of Rebecca. I hoped she'd been received by the Virgin with a loving embrace and was at peace.

* * *

JUNE 9

My brother came late in the afternoon today. Jimmy was with him.

"Hey, cutie!"

That's how Jimmy always greeted me. His reddish-blond hair and freckles announced to the world he was of Scottish decent. They added to his air of joy, and I smiled. They both kissed me and then took seats.

"Do you want to see my new marking?" I asked. "The Virgin showed me the other night."

Eddie and Jimmy glanced at each other.

"Elena, that's why we're here," my brother said. "We want to talk to you about the markings."

"Well, look then." And with pride, I rolled up my sleeve and showed them what I'd done with the plastic fork.

Jimmy's eyes went wide. "Jesus, Mary, and Joseph."

Eddie traced the new symbol with his finger. Then he and Jimmy exchanged glances again.

"What?" I asked. "You keep looking at each other."

"Elena, I recognized the first two markings in the photos Eddie showed me," Jimmy said. "And now that I see the third, I know you haven't made them up. I'm sure of what they are. They form a word."

He reached into his backpack and pulled out photocopy of a page from some book. I scrunched my face as I studied the paper.

לחמ

"What is it?" I asked.

"It's ancient Aramaic," Jimmy said.

"Aramaic?"

Jimmy nodded. "What's on your arm, those markings, they represent the language of Jesus. And of the Virgin Mary."

I still didn't understand.

"Ancient Aramaic is a form of old Hebrew," Jimmy said. "It was spoken in the Middle East during the time of Jesus."

I glanced at Eddie. He gestured at Jimmy with a head tilt. "Go ahead. Tell her."

"These three symbols are letters. You read from right to left. They form a word: *rachem*."

I furrowed my brow. "What does that mean?"

"In the language of Jesus, it means something like 'mercy' or 'love,' depending on the context." Jimmy shook his head. "I don't know how, but someone or something is communicating with you through the language of Jesus."

"Sweetie," Eddie said, "it's not possible you would know Aramaic. It's a good thing Jimmy here studies such things." He leaned over and kissed his boyfriend on the cheek.

"Eduardo! How dare you!"

We all turned toward the doorway. My father stood there, rigid, my mother right behind him. He jutted his chin toward Jimmy.

"And what is *he* doing here?"

"Papá," I said. "They're just here for a visit. Please, let them—"

"Don't tell me what to do!" His voice boomed against the walls of my small room. He took several steps toward us. "You are my daughter and what I say goes!"

"I am your daughter, yes." My tone had risen. "But I am not your property!"

I trembled slightly at my own audacity. My mother put her hand to her mouth as tears flowed. But I pushed on.

"Eddie is here, and I want him to stay. He makes me feel good. So does Jimmy. They both love me. And isn't it important that I feel good, here in this clinic where you've put me?" My reproach shot across the room like a cannon ball.

"E…E…Elena…" My father's tongue tripped on my name.

"I'm sorry," I continued. "Truly, I am. But only Eddie and Jimmy understand what I'm experiencing. Everybody else wants to judge me, administer treatment because they think I'm crazy. They want to mold me, put me in some box with the label 'good daughter' or 'cured.'"

My father's eyes had become slits, and I could feel the mix of surprise and anger that emanated from them.

"Papá, please." I felt tears forming but I pushed them back. I wouldn't allow myself to cry. "You have to understand that I know who I am. And my life is my life. If I say the Virgin talks to me, it's because she does."

My father trembled as his hands curled into fists. My mother sobbed and said nothing.

"Elena," he said, "I'm telling you. If you don't stop behaving—"

"Behaving how?" Eddie said. He stood, defiant in his posture—his shoulders pulled back, his chest thrust forward. "Don't you see that something...something important is happening to Elena?"

They stared at each other, not sure of what the other might say or do. My father's face twisted into a reddened grimace. Spittle gathered at the corner of his mouth. He shook violently, and then collapsed to the floor. My mother screamed. Eddie crouched beside him. Jimmy charged out the door calling for help.

I pushed myself off the bed. "Papá?" But a voice wove its way into my thoughts. A female voice. I recognized it right away.

Quiet, my dear. Quiet. All is fine. All is fine.

I looked at the scene in front of me. My mother weeping, my father limp and cradled in Jimmy's arms. I heard commotion in the hallway. I felt dizzy and placed my hand on the bed to steady myself. The room seemed to tilt sideways as it faded away.

Then everything went black.

• • •

JUNE 10

I don't know how many hours I slept but it seems like a lot. I woke up this morning and Eddie was seated next to my bed. He smiled at me.

"How are you feeling, sweetie?"

"Okay, I guess. But...where's Dad?"

He brushed my forehead. "Don't worry. He's fine. He suffered a minor heart attack, they say he'll be okay with rest and some good home care. Mom is with him."

"Eddie, I feel so bad. I didn't mean to cause—"

He put a finger to my lips. "Stop. I know what you're going to say. You didn't do anything. It was something physical, something inside Dad. You know he doesn't take care of himself, that he doesn't eat right or exercise. And with his temper, well, sooner or later his health would suffer."

"But—"

"No 'buts,'" he said. "You can't feel guilty for something out of your control."

Just then, Jimmy waltzed in.

"Hey, cutie." He leaned in and kissed me. "Sorry. I was out parking the car." He pulled a small package from his backpack. "Eddie and I have a present for you. Happy birthday!"

"Happy birthday," Eddie added.

I grinned. "That's right! I completely forgot!"

Jimmy pointed to the gift in my hands. "Well, what are you waiting for?"

I unwrapped the box and opened it to find a small gold necklace. Suspended in the middle was a small pendant with the word *Love*.

"It's beautiful!" I dangled it from my fingers.

"We bought it the other day," Jimmy said. "And now that we know what you've been marking on your arm, well, it just all seems to fit."

"Love. *Rachem*." I pronounced the words slowly, and then added, "Mercy."

Eddie reached for the necklace. "Let's see how it looks on you." He secured it around my neck. "There. It's perfect."

"Oh, thank you, Eddie. Thank you, Jimmy." I hugged them both.

Eddie twisted his mouth slightly and rubbed his nose. "Uh, Elena, there's something I want to talk to you about."

I caressed the pendant. "What?"

"You're eighteen. You're legally an adult. You don't have to stay here if you don't want to."

"Yeah, Elena." Jimmy sat on the edge of the bed. "I made some phone calls this morning. You don't need anyone's consent if you want to leave."

The reminder hit me like lightning. Relief washed over me. But it didn't last. I lowered my gaze.

"Dad…"

Eddie sighed. "I told you. He's going to be fine. Everything is fine."

And then I remembered what the Virgin said to me yesterday: *Quiet, my dear. Quiet. All is fine. All is fine.*

I drew in a deep breath. "Okay. Who do I talk to?"

Jimmy jumped up. "I'll go find out." He hurried out of the room.

I looked at my brother. "I really like Jimmy."

"I know." He reached down and took my hands in his. "Can I tell you something?"

"Anything."

"He's asked me to marry him."

I almost burst. I threw my arms around his neck.

"That's wonderful! I'm so happy!" I pulled back and wiped away a tear.

"But I have no idea how Mom and Dad will react," he said. He looked away and then down. "I don't think Dad could take it right now…"

I clasped his hand and squeezed gently. "Don't worry. You'll see. Dad will come around. I'll work on him for you."

I winked and that made him smile.

"I'm so excited," I said with a squeal.

I thought about my father. *Yes, yes. He'll come around.* I caressed the pendant once more.

Love. Mercy. Rachem.

* * *

JUNE 24

I've been home for two weeks now. The Virgin hasn't come to me since I left the clinic. I lie in my bed waiting for midnight, but all is silent. I miss her and I wonder if she'll ever come back.

My father was released two days after I left the clinic, and like Eddie said, if he takes care of himself and watches what he eats, he should be fine. In fact, the doctor said he could have a long, good life. The heart attack scared him to no end, though. I think it pushed him to reconsider a few things. We talked as though we hadn't argued that day in the hospital, and I was able to tell him about many things, including what happened to Rebecca.

"We never wanted that to happen to you," he said. He lifted my hand and kissed the back of it gently. "You are good daughter, a good person. It makes me happy we are back in this house together."

I told him about the markings and what they turned out to mean.

"Do you believe now what I said all along?" I asked.

"What's important," he said, "is that you believe. Never stop believing in the power of God."

I smiled, knowing that would be the best answer he would ever give. Maybe someday, the Virgin would speak to him. I asked him why he was so upset with Eddie, why he couldn't just love him and accept him.

"M'hija," he said, "I do love him. I just listened to all the wrong people. Father González, friends, coworkers. I should have listened to my heart." His eyes moistened. "He has the same blood in his veins as you, as me and your mom. The same blood as Ernesto."

He paused and for a moment, and he seemed to slip away, his thoughts on the past. Then he looked at me once more.

"He is family."

After two years of not visiting, Eddie finally came down to Mañana. Standing in the kitchen, with the smell of cooking beans on the stove and fresh tortillas in the air, he told our parents he was engaged. There was a pause as my dad looked at him. Then he shuffled to Eddie and pulled him into his arms.

"If you're happy," he said, "then I'm happy for you."

We all sat at the table as Eddie told us about their future plans. My mother clapped with delight at the thought of planning a wedding.

"We'll have the reception at the golf course," she said. "They have a beautiful garden outside the restaurant. Oh, I can see it now! A fall wedding, just when the weather turns. We'll do it right before the sun sets."

She kissed Eddie on the top of his head and then bustled about the kitchen getting lunch ready. Eddie chuckled at seeing her so animated.

"Why didn't Jimmy come with you?" my father asked.

"Well, uh, Papá..."

"Call him," Dad said. "Tell him to come down. He is going to be part of the family."

Eddie teared up. "You know I love you, right?"

My dad smiled and patted Eddie's hand.

The Virgin was right. Everything is fine.

I don't know if I'll continue writing in my journal. There's no psychologist to tell me I should do it. So, this may very well be the last page I ever write. Here, anyway, and about this time in my life. I'll finish by saying what I said from the outset.

I'm not crazy. I'm not sick. I never was.

And I'll add the following: I truly believe that everything is possible in life. We simply need to open up our hearts. That's what the Virgin wanted me to understand and why she had me mark my skin. The symbols will live with me forever. I know now she wants me to spread the word. That will be my mission in life.

Love.
Mercy.
Rachem.

Acknowledgements

'd like to thank Mark Spencer for his help and guidance. His continued encouragement has meant a lot to me. I also need to thank my friends in The Writerie and Chowchilla writing group—Glenna, Bob, Ramona, Wyatt, and Sharon. Also, thanks to Sheila and Terry for reading and commenting on various stories. The support of friends is always welcome. Special thanks go to Kevin Breen, my editor, who reviewed, commented on, and offered wonderful suggestions. Thanks are also due to Steve Kuhn for his wonderful cover and interior design and layout. Jesse Coleman, you did a great job in the final editing to catch all my mistakes and offering additional suggestions. Thank you. Finally, I need to thank all the readers out there. You make it all worthwhile.

About the Author

Bill VanPatten is the author of four novels: *Seidon's Tale*, recipient of the Klops-Fetherling Silver Phoenix Award for new voices in fiction in 2019; *Looks Are Deceiving: A Will Christian Mystery*; *A Little* Rain; and *Sometimes You Just* Know. He is also the author of two collections of short stories—*Dust Storm: Stories from Lubbock* and *The Whisper of Clouds: Stories from the Windy City*. He also writes fiction in Spanish for heritage speakers and second language learners. He left a very successful career in academia to pursue both fiction and nonfiction writing and currently lives in the Central Valley of California. *There Go I* is his third collection of short stories. You can find out more about him at www.billvanpatten.net.

Made in the USA
Middletown, DE
03 October 2022